Montana's Way

Montana's Way

Sheila M. Goss

www.urbanbooks.net

Urban Books, LLC
300 Farmingdale Road, NY-Route 109
Farmingdale, NY 11735

Montana's Way
Copyright © 2019 Sheila M. Goss

ISBN 13: 978-1-60162-863-3
ISBN 10: 1-60162-863-3

First Mass Market Printing March 2019
First Trade Paperback Printing December 2012
Printed in the United States of America

10 9 8 7 6 5 4 3 2 1

Distributed by Kensington Publishing Corp.
Submit Orders to:
Customer Service
400 Hahn Road
Westminster, MD 21157-4627
Phone: 1-800-733-3000
Fax: 1-800-659-2436

I thank my Heavenly Father for the lessons and the blessings.

I dedicate this book to my mother, Exie Goss. Thank you for being there during not only the good times, but the bad times. I appreciate all of the love and support from my close friends and family.

This marks my tenth anniversary in this industry. I want to thank everyone for spreading the word about my books. I appreciate you all. Thank you, readers!

Shelia M. Goss

~ 1 ~

Rain hitting against the window ledge sounded like music to twenty-nine-year-old Montana Blake's ears. She lazily lay on her queen-sized pillow-top mattress and read the *Dallas Morning News* headline, COMMANDER RAYMOND STEEL RECEIVES LIFE.

She smiled as she thought about her sisters, Savannah and Asia. Closure was what they sought when it came to the death of their father, Major Blake, and that's exactly what they got. Thanks to the help of Savannah's fiancé, Troy Bridges, justice had been served. It had taken a little over two years, but the man responsible for their father's death would now be serving a life sentence.

Montana reached for her iPhone on the cherry-wood nightstand. Before she could dial the first digit, her baby sister Asia's kilowatt smile flashed across the screen.

"Did you see it? It's over. It's finally over," Asia squealed from the other end with glee.

"Finally. . . ." Montana's voice trailed off as she listened to Asia go on and on about the trials and tribulations of the last few years.

Montana's initial loyalty to their Uncle Raymond almost cost them their lives, but after learning he was responsible for their dad's death, Montana, like her two sisters, was determined to prove his guilt. Instead of killing him like he did their father, they decided to let the justice system work. With the mounting evidence against Raymond, who was once considered their father's best friend, he was tried and convicted and sentenced to life. Life without parole. And, now, Montana and her sisters could move forward with their lives.

"Earth to Montana," Asia said several times.

"My mind was a million miles away," Montana responded.

"Now, maybe we can convince our sister to go ahead and say 'I do' to Troy."

Troy and Savannah got engaged shortly after Raymond was arrested, but Savannah insisted on them waiting until the trial was over before proceeding. Savannah could be stubborn, just like each one of the Blake sisters.

"Maybe there's more to it than she's telling us." Montana would back Savannah's choice, regardless.

"She loves Troy and Troy loves her. If they can withstand all of this, then their relationship can survive anything."

Montana agreed. "Have you talked to her this morning?"

"No, I was going to ask you the same thing," Asia responded.

"Hold on." Montana dialed Savannah's number. She was surprised that Savannah hadn't called either her or Asia by now. They had all learned of Raymond's fate the day before but to see it in black and white somehow made it official. Montana couldn't wait to celebrate with Savannah. She clicked back over. "The phone keeps going to voice mail."

Asia said, "Hold on, I'll try Troy's number."

Montana kept dialing Savannah's house number and cell number while waiting for Asia to return. "Still no answer," Montana said out loud.

"No luck with Troy either," Asia responded.

Montana glanced at the clock. "Meet me at their place in about forty minutes. It'll take me about fifteen to get dressed."

Asia and Montana ended their call. Montana jumped out of the bed. Making up the bed was part of her normal morning routine but this morning she was more concerned about getting in contact with Savannah. The clothes in her walk-in closet were color coordinated so, after taking a quick shower, it didn't take her long in picking something to wear. She zipped up her green slacks and pulled on her lime-green blouse before pulling her jet-black hair into a ponytail.

Montana's mind drifted to Uncle Raymond as she drove to Savannah's. His unexpected betrayal still left a bitter taste in Montana's mouth. She felt guilty for believing that he was really there to help them. Her misguided allegiance jeopardized her sisters lives. She would no longer take their lives for granted and would do anything to protect their livelihood.

After almost forty minutes exactly, she was pulling her black SUV behind Asia's red sports car in Savannah and Troy's circular driveway. Montana eased out of her vehicle with her cell phone in one hand and keys in the other. She placed them both in her pants pocket. Asia startled her when Asia's door flew open.

"I was just trying to call you," Asia said as she ran her hand through her cropped sandy-brown hair and exited her car.

"I bet you her and Troy are getting their groove on," Montana said as they walked past both Troy's and Savannah's vehicles.

"I'm surprised the gate wasn't closed."

Montana reached the front door first. She reached down and rang the doorbell next to the huge door attached to the two-story custom-made house.

Asia pulled out her cell phone. They could hear the phone ringing. There was no answer from the door, nor the phone. "Let me find my key and code because they should be able to see we're out here," Asia said as she fumbled through her purse.

Montana barely touched the doorknob when the door flew open. "That's odd," Montana said out loud as the door opened.

Asia pushed past Montana and called out, "Savannah . . . Troy."

"I'll check downstairs, you check upstairs," Montana said as she followed Asia inside.

With the gate being opened and the door not locked, Montana felt it in her gut that something wasn't right. Even if the gate was opened, the front door was always locked. If Savannah and Troy were going to be away, they would forward their house phone to their cell phone. Things were out of sync. The lack of sound in the house was eerie. Montana stopped dead in her tracks when she heard Asia scream. Montana skipped stairs as she rushed toward the sound of Asia's voice.

The king-sized pillow-top bed covers were thrown on the floor, with drops of blood on the floor. Other than the disheveled look of the bed, it was hard to tell that an intruder had been present.

"Montana, something's happened," Asia kept repeating over and over.

"Don't touch anything. We need to leave the room exactly like we found it," Montana said as her heart rate increased. She took a few deep breaths in attempts to ease her nerves so she could remain calm.

Asia's face turned beet red. "I see blood. You don't think—"

"Don't even say it," Montana said, as she retrieved her cell phone and dialed 911. "I'm at 7845 Wilshire Lane."

The operator asked, "What's the nature of your emergency?"

"My sister and her fiancé are missing."

"Ma'am. When you say missing . . . what do you mean?"

"We've been trying to reach my sister for an hour. There's blood and we haven't been able to reach them. Please send an officer here right away."

"Please don't touch anything and for your safety, you may want to wait for the officers in your car," the operator responded.

Montana hung up the phone. She grabbed Asia by the arm. "We need to get out of here just in case whoever did this comes back."

"I'm not going anywhere. We need to look through this before the cops get here and see if we can find anything that will help tell us what happened."

Montana threw her hands up in the air. "You and Savannah need to stop with the Nancy Drew–type stuff. Didn't you get enough of this with the Uncle Raymond situation?"

"Of course, but this is our sister. We can't trust the police to care about her the way we do."

"I know, but still, Asia. We're not experts. Troy is the expert."

"Fine. I'll call Mike. He'll know what to do."

"I thought you didn't like Mike. You both seemed to bump heads when he gave us extensive self-defense training," Montana stated.

"If he wasn't such a jerk, he would make someone a good husband." Asia held her hand up to indicate she had him on the phone. "Mike, we need you to get to Troy's place pronto. He and Savannah are missing and there's blood."

Montana paced back and forth in front of the bedroom doorway. The last time Savannah and Troy faced danger it was because Raymond was behind it. Raymond was behind bars. Could he be reaching out beyond the bars? So many questions went back and forth in Montana's head.

"He's on his way. He said, 'Do not touch anything.' He wished we would have called him before the police," Asia stated as she placed the phone in her pocket.

"I wish we didn't have to call anyone." Montana wrapped her arms around herself. "The police will be here any minute. Hopefully, they can find out something."

Montana knew enough from her listening to her father that they shouldn't touch anything in the room that may tamper with evidence. Asia and Montana went together to search the other rooms upstairs. Nothing else seemed to be out of order.

With Troy and Savannah living in an affluent neighborhood, it wasn't a surprise to Montana that it didn't take long for the police to arrive. The front doorbell rang. "That should be the police," Asia said, but she retrieved a small handgun from her ankle and pulled it out just in case.

"Is that really necessary?" Montana asked.

"Duh. Just in case it isn't the police." Asia led them both down the stairs.

The silhouette of two policemen could be seen through the stained-glass windows on each side of the door. Montana looked out the peephole to make sure. She saw two police officers and two patrol cars outside. She opened the door.

"We received a nine-one-one emergency call from this address," the tall, dark, and handsome officer said.

Montana moved to the side. She glanced, and the gun that Asia had out was no longer in view. "We think someone's abducted my sister and her fiancé."

The petite female officer asked, "Whose house is this?"

"It's theirs," Asia responded.

"And who are you?" the female officer asked.

"I'm Asia. My sister is the one who's missing."

Montana explained to the officer, "We've been unable to reach my sister Savannah. Which is unlike her, to not reach out to either one of us. We drove over here and didn't have to use our key. We found blood upstairs."

Both of the officers followed Asia up the stairs. Montana followed them. The officers surveyed the bedroom.

"Jenkins, we might need to call backup," the female officer said.

"I've handled enough of these cases. If I need help, I know how to ask for it," Jenkins snapped.

Montana didn't have time for what appeared to be rivalry between the two. "I don't care who handles it. I need for you, or someone, to tell me what happened to my sister."

The female officer said, "Normally, we don't take a missing person's report until someone has been missing for more than twenty-four hours."

Jenkins interrupted, "But since it appears there was some foul play involved, we're going to do whatever we can now."

"This is why we think something happened," Asia said.

The doorbell rang again. Jenkins asked, "Were you expecting anyone?"

Montana glanced past them at Asia. "Yes, friends of the owner. I'll be back in a few."

Montana peeped out the peephole and saw Mike and the back of someone else. She pulled the door open. "Mike, I'm scared."

Montana let out all of the bottled-up emotions of fear and flew into Mike's arms. He did his best to comfort her. Mike patted her on the back. "We're going to find them."

She forgot that Mike wasn't alone. The sight of a familiar face was all Montana needed to pull herself together. She brushed the tears from her face and stared at the cold, black, piercing eyes staring back.

Sean Patterson stood speechless as the object of his dreams now stood right there before him. He happened to be in Mike's office when he received the call from Asia about Troy and Savannah's disappearance. It only took them seconds to reach Mike's car and they drove as fast as the Dallas morning traffic would allow them to Troy's place.

Montana's tall stature was still no match for his six-foot-two-inch frame. The vulnerability he saw when she was rescued three years ago from her psycho ex-boyfriend was the same look she now possessed. Montana was unaware of Sean's instant attraction to her. Sean wasn't even too sure that Montana even knew his name but yet, he knew everything about her. The gleam in Montana's eyes disappeared as he stared back.

Mike broke the silence between Sean and Montana. "Montana, not sure if you remember

Sean, but he's one of the partners. He works with Troy and I. He's going to assist me."

"You can rest assured that we're going to do whatever needs to be done to find out your sister and Troy's whereabouts," Sean stated in his deep baritone voice.

Montana, barely above a whisper, said, "Thank you. Thank you, both. The police are upstairs with Asia now."

"I'll check things out down here," Sean said as Mike went upstairs.

Having helped Troy set up security for his house, Sean knew the house like he knew his own. He used his own personal key to open up the secret door that led to the basement. He typed in the security code and the lights turned on. The basement held state-of-the-art electronic equipment that included surveillance monitors and an arsenal of weapons.

Sean sat behind one of the monitors and rewound the digital tape twenty-four hours. He smiled as he saw Troy and Savannah enter the house. They appeared to be so much in love. He fast-forwarded the tape until nightfall. That's when he noticed some shadow figures approaching the lawn. They were all dressed in black jumpsuits with black masks. No sounds could be heard. One was using hand signals to the others as they broke through the security gate and surrounded the house. That's when everything went completely dark.

There were no cameras in Troy and Savannah's bedroom, but there was no need because Sean got a clear view of the assailants as they assembled in the hallway. He zoomed in on the duck tattoo on one of the assailants' hands. It was the same tattoo some of the other assailants had on their hands. A total of five assailants were seen on the screen.

Troy tried to save himself and Savannah by fighting them off but to no avail. He was clearly outnumbered. It angered Sean to watch a bloodied Troy and a reluctant Savannah dragged out by several of the assailants. Savannah seemed to be unharmed. Troy looked in the direction where he knew there was a camera and mouthed the word "Driskoll."

Sean stopped the tape and rewound it to make sure he read Troy's lips correctly. Time was ticking. If Driskoll was their kidnapper, time was not on their side. Sean downloaded the information on one of the flash drives near the computer and left the hidden room, undetected.

Montana paced back and forth in the kitchen. "Where were you? We were looking for you. Well, I was looking for you," she said.

"I was checking the surveillance room Troy has set up in the basement to see if I could see any signs of what happened. I think I've found something."

"Sir, and who are you?" A tall police officer entered the room.

Sean extended his hand. "I'm Sean Patterson. Troy Bridges is my business partner. We would really like the police's cooperation as we try to figure out Troy's location."

"Patterson that is. Well, leave the investigating to the pros."

"No disrespect, Officer."

"That's Detective. Detective Jenkins."

"Detective Jenkins, I think it's in both of our best interests to work together."

Jenkins's forehead drew up. "We got this."

Montana interrupted. "Look. I don't care who does what. All I want is my sister back with me safe and sound."

Sean ran into people like Jenkins all the time. Jenkins thought he was the next Columbo but, in actuality, Troy and Savannah were dead if they relied on Jenkins alone. Sean knew he had to play the game so he backed off. "We're here to help in any way." Sean retrieved a business card from his pocket and handed it to Jenkins.

Jenkins turned to Montana. "If you can think of anything else, let me know. I think we took enough pictures and gathered up enough evidence for now."

Montana's hands flew up in the air. "Is that it? Man, I could have done a better job than that."

"Ms. Blake, we still don't know if they were abducted. Unless you get a phone call or something, we're just not sure. Me and my partner will ask some of the neighbors to see if they saw anything suspicious."

"Yes, you do that."

Sean would do anything to erase the frustration from Montana's face. She followed the officer out of the kitchen. Sean glanced at the flash drive in the palm of his hand. He debated whether to tell Montana what he'd discovered.

"Losing your concentration already," Mike said from behind him.

Sean turned around and saw that Mike wasn't by himself. Asia, who now wore her hair in a cropped hair style, reminding him of a younger version of Halle Berry, walked right behind Mike.

"You remember Asia?" Mike asked.

"I sure do. The woman who got a bull's eye on the moving target ten times in a row."

Asia pointed her finger and blew the tip. "And don't you ever forget it either."

They all laughed, although it was tense.

"I'm glad you all can find something funny because if we have to rely on Barney Fife and his sidekick, we're in some deep trouble," Asia said.

Sean made his decision then. "Follow me."

They all followed Sean to Troy's office. Sean turned the computer on and typed in his login and password. He inserted the flash drive. "Okay, ladies, what you see here might not be pretty but you need to see this so you'll know how serious this is."

Sean moved and let Montana sit in the leather chair behind the computer. He watched the shocked expressions on their faces as they heard the scuffle going on in the bedroom. He saw the relieved look when they saw Savannah walking out unharmed.

Mike was the first to speak. "You two have a decision to make. We can turn over this information to the police and let them handle it—"

Sean interrupted, "Or you can trust us." He looked at Mike and then at Montana and Asia. "And let us handle this. I promise you, I will risk my life to save my brother Troy's and Savannah's lives."

Montana looked at Asia and then back at Sean. "Let us discuss and we'll let you know."

"Montana, you saw the detective. My toy poodle would be more capable of finding Troy than him."

"Man, you have a toy poodle?" Mike asked.

Sean ignored him. "Trust me. Trust Mike."

"Give us ten minutes," Montana said.

~ 3 ~

As soon as Mike and Sean were out of the room, Asia said, "What is there to think about? I sure in the hell trust Mike more than I trust that cop trying to play detective. He didn't even ask if there were any security cameras. A house this big . . . that's the first thing I would have asked."

"But, what can they do? Troy was the one with the connections. Mike and Sean just work for him."

"Sis, you don't know anything. Sean is Troy's silent partner. Sean is the one who sets up a lot of the operations in the field. Sean's risked his life to retrieve kidnap victims all over the world."

"And how do you know this?"

"Because Mike told me. If anyone can get Vanna back safe, it's Sean."

Montana scratched her head. "Asia, I don't know about this. The police have teams in place to handle situations like this. We can show them the tape and then see what happens."

"Look. I'm going to say this once. You can go work with the police but for me, I'm with Mike and Sean. I'm not taking any chances. You saw how they brushed our dad's case to the side."

"I know, but still, Asia, Troy was the one who was instrumental in finding out who killed our dad."

"I'm not going to keep going back and forth with you on this . . . don't have time . . . time that could be better used on Sean and Mike discovering where Troy and Vanna are."

Montana rushed out of the room behind Asia. "Wait. I'm not going to let you do this without me."

"Then I suggest you come aboard because I'm going to work with them to find our sister, with or without you."

As much as Montana didn't really want to go along with Asia, she refused to let her go about it alone. She had lost one sister, she wasn't about to lose another. They needed to stick together now more than ever. "Fine. I'm with you. Tell them to do whatever they need to do."

"No, we're going to do whatever we need to do. If I have to go undercover, we're getting them back."

That's exactly what Montana was afraid of. Asia could be hotheaded. She needed to be around to make sure Asia didn't do anything stupid.

Sean and Mike were found upstairs going through the bedroom. They each had a forensic kit. They dusted for fingerprints and took blood samples. Sean looked up in Montana's direction. "I doubt if we'll find any fingerprints. The assailants wore gloves, but because the cameras weren't in this room, we can never be so sure."

"Did you happen to find Savannah's cell phone?" Asia asked.

"No, it's missing, but we found Troy's still on the floor near the nightstand," Mike responded.

"I know you got tracking devices. Vanna's number is 972-555-2567," Asia blurted out.

Mike said, "See why I like her? She's not just a pretty face."

Asia rolled her eyes. "Whatever. Use your device and we might be able to track where they are."

Sean said, "Mike, you finish up here and I'll go log on the computer downstairs and see what I can make happen."

"I'm going with you," Asia stated.

Montana stayed behind with Mike. "So, how well do you know this Sean?"

Mike continued to log things into his hand-held device. "Me, Sean, and Troy all started off at the agency together. You could say we all got tired of working for the SNA when too many of our comrades started getting killed and no one seemed to give a damn about it."

"I heard Troy talking about it."

"Sean's one of the good guys. Troy and Sean are like brothers. Troy and Sean's been knowing each other since college. Both have similar backgrounds. Put it like this, I would rather work with Sean than against him."

"Oh and why is that?"

"'Cause, when he sets his mind on something, he usually gets it." Mike winked his eye.

Montana felt a little uncomfortable but didn't say anything. She looked under the bed to see if they overlooked finding Savannah's cell phone. Still nothing.

"Well, I'm through up here. Let's go see if they were able to track Savannah's phone."

Montana responded, "Give me a minute. I'll be down."

Montana did something she should have done the moment she realized Savannah was missing. She dropped to her knees and prayed. "God, please put your arm of protection around Savannah and Troy and deliver them safely back to us."

Shortly thereafter, she walked downstairs to see if there was any good news.

"Good. I won't have to repeat myself," Sean said. "I just got a call from one of our workers. It's been confirmed who has Troy and Savannah. I wasn't able to locate Savannah's phone from this computer so I'm waiting to hear from the office."

"Who has them?" Asia asked.

Sean looked at Mike. Montana didn't like the intense looks shared between the two of them. "Spill it out," Montana said.

"It's an underground organization that has infiltrated several businesses, some look legit but are financed with money made from the sale of illegal drugs and weapons. I was instrumental in taking one of their key men out. They kidnapped Troy to get to me."

"But, I don't understand. You're not blood brothers, so why Troy?"

"People like this know how to find out information. Anyone who knows me knows there's nothing I wouldn't do for Troy. Troy is closer to me than a blood brother. That's why it's so important to me to find out where he is so I can get him out safely."

Montana thought she saw his eyes water. She wanted to reach out to him and hug him.

"What's next? I feel like we're just sitting around wasting time," Asia blurted.

"Calm down," Mike said.

"Y'all have to excuse Asia. I'm the calm one."

"Montana, please, let's not go there. You're the biggest drama queen."

Sean's cell phone ringing interrupted the sister banter. "It's a blocked number." Sean held his hand up, motioning for them to be quiet.

Montana mouthed words to Asia. Asia shifted in her seat, sat back, and crossed her arms.

Sean wrote something down on a piece of paper and hung up the phone. "They've been located. Savannah must have her phone on her. Good thing you thought of it before her battery went dead," Sean said.

"Well, what are y'all sitting around for? Go get my sister," Montana shouted.

"I'm going to need your help. I understand you can transform a person's look."

"Yes, but how is that going to help?" Montana asked.

"I need to be transformed, because if I go in looking like this Troy and Savannah are as good as dead."

Montana looked at Sean. "Making over some-one is my specialty. I used to work on movie sets. Everything I need is at my place."

"Can I hitch a ride? I rode with Mike."

"Come on," Montana said as she got up and rushed out the door.

~ 4 ~

Sean leaned to the side, thankful that he
had his seatbelt on as Montana dodged in and
out of traffic toward her house. She lived thirty
minutes away in normal time but she got them
there in less than twenty minutes.

"This is the house we grew up in," Montana
said as she unlocked the door.

"Nice."

"I like it. I got it when Savannah decided to
move in with Troy. Now I'm not so sure it was a
good idea."

"Trust me, Troy would risk his life to save
Savannah's. So, no worries."

"But what if Troy's already dead? What's going
to happen to her?"

"I like to focus on the positive."

"Sure. Have a seat at the table. I'll be right
back," Montana responded.

Sean scanned the den and admired the African
motif. He was sure some of the paintings and

hand carvings were probably authentic and not duplicates. Being in this house made Sean recall memories of Montana's dad, Major. Everything he learned about serving and protecting his country and those he loved he learned from Major. Major was the ultimate super soldier.

"I know you like those dreads, but in order to transform your look, those are going to have to go." Montana pulled her hand from behind her back and held some clippers.

"These are my strength," Sean stated. "Do you know how long it took me to grow these out?"

"No, but if you want me to transform you into someone else, you must trust me."

Sean grunted. "Trust you. Do you trust me?"

Montana remained silent.

Sean said, "That's what I thought."

Montana plugged in the clippers. "It's not that I don't trust you. I don't really know you. Mike trusts you and apparently Troy trusted you, so I'm going to take my chances."

"So what you're saying is I should take my chances on you?"

Montana turned the clippers on. The roaring sound of the clippers filled the air. "Exactly. Now, sit back and watch me work."

Sean cringed with each fall of one of his locks. "I can't believe I'm letting you do this."

"Believe it and you'll like it. I can already see the difference."

"So what are you saying? You don't like a man with locks?"

"I'm not saying a word," Montana playfully teased.

"Can you hurry up? We don't want them to move from that location."

"Do you want me to do this or should I let you finish it up."

"Okay. I'll be quiet," Sean said.

"Good."

Montana handed Sean a mirror when she finished. "Wow. I don't even look like myself."

Sean ran his hand over his now close cut hair. He felt completely naked with all of his hair now on the floor beside him.

"I know. And, now, the eyebrows."

"Oh. Now see, that's where I draw the line. You are not going to cut off my eyebrows."

"I'm just arching them." Montana removed a razor from her small handbag. "Now lean back."

Sean did as he was told. "Be gentle."

"I'll try," Montana responded.

When she was through, Sean stood up.

Montana said, "I'm not finished. I need to lighten you up. This makeup will not wipe off. It'll take several different applicators to wipe this off you."

"This is enough. I don't need any makeup."

"Who's the expert, you or me?"

"You are."

"Then I suggest you sit." Montana was in her zone, Sean could tell.

When Montana finished with the make-up, she placed some brown contacts in his eyes. He looked at the mirror and he looked like a totally different person. He was several shades lighter than his normal brown complexion. "Good job."

"I'll bill you."

"What's your number? I will call you and let you know when we have them."

"Oh no, I'm not staying here. I'm going with you."

"Look, I don't have time to argue with you. This is not a safe mission and if you go with me, I'm going to be too concerned with your safety. I need to concentrate on the task at hand."

"So you're saying you can't concentrate around me," Montana said.

"That's exactly what I'm saying," Sean said, not having time to deny it. Sean looked at his cell phone. The text message indicated his ride was outside.

"Why is that?"

Sean got caught up in the moment and pulled Montana closer to him and kissed her with a passion he didn't know he possessed. Time stood still between the two of them. He released her. "I'm sorry. I need to go. I didn't mean to."

Montana wrote something down on a piece of paper. "Here's my number. But I want to be in the car. I promise not to get out."

"You're safer here. I'll call you. Promise."

Without giving Montana time to protest, Sean rushed out of her house into the waiting black sedan with some of his comrades.

"Man, I almost didn't recognize you," Mike said as Sean slipped in the back seat beside him.

"I almost didn't recognize myself."

~ 5 ~

Not long after Sean left, Asia appeared. "This waiting is killing me," Montana, who was normally the calm one, said as she paced back and forth in front of Asia, who sat on the couch using her iPad.

"I prayed on the way over here. What did Dad teach us? We have to have faith," Asia said.

"I prayed too, but I'm still scared. If anything happened to Vanna, I don't know. . . ." Montana's voice trailed off.

"Don't even go there. Sean's going to call you, or Mike's going to call me with good news any minute now."

Montana needed to do something to get her mind off things. She had already cleaned up the living room where she had cut Sean's hair, so she did what she did when she couldn't rest: she went to the kitchen and started looking through the pantry and refrigerator to cook.

"I can't even think about food right now," Asia said as she wandered in.

"I need to do something. What do you want? Brownies? A cake?"

"I don't care."

Montana put on a kitchen apron with her name on it and took out the ingredients she needed to make some brownies. Cooking had always been Montana's stress relieving mechanism. With everything going on, her sister's disappearance, the unsuspected feelings for Sean that seemed to come out of nowhere, Montana needed something to calm her nerves.

Montana's cell phone rang. "Asia, can you get that for me?" She held her hands up. There was brownie mix on them.

"Where's your speaker button?" Asia asked frantically.

"Top button."

"Vanna, you okay?" Asia yelled.

"Look, I only have one bar left. I don't know where I'm at, but try to trace my phone."

"Vanna, this is Asia. Montana's here. Mike and Sean got your location. Help is on the way."

"Thank God. They've beat up Troy real bad."

"And you . . . What about you?" Montana asked. She was glued to her spot.

"I'm fine . . . for now."

Montana didn't like the sound of that but she tried to stay strong. "Keep your ears open. They will be making their move anytime."

"They just took Troy to another room. I'm scared something bad is about to happen to him."

Montana could hear the fear in Savannah's voice. "Hang on in there, sis. We need you, so you got to come back home to us."

"I love y'all. Somebody's coming. Got to go."

"Love you too," Asia and Montana said but the phone had already disconnected.

Montana spoke out first. "I don't have Sean's number. Call Mike and tell him what just happened."

Asia was already dialing Mike's number. Asia sighed. "He's not picking up."

"Do you happen to know where they were going?" Montana asked.

"As a matter of fact, I do," Asia responded.

"Are you thinking what I'm thinking?" Montana turned the stove off and placed the brownie mix in the refrigerator.

"Mike said we should stay out of it," Asia said.

"And when do you listen to anyone?" Montana responded as she removed the apron. Before Asia could say anything, Montana was upstairs in her closet retrieving two pair of black jeans and black T-shirts.

Asia walked in. "You know your clothes are too big for me."

Montana threw a pair of black jeans at Asia. "These are your size, Ms. Shorty."

Asia rolled her eyes. "I'm only a few inches shorter."

"I know. That's why I know these will fit. Hurry up."

"I can't believe I'm going along with this," Asia said as she took off her clothes and replaced them with the black jeans and T-shirt.

"Do you have your gun with you?" Montana asked.

"Right here." Asia patted her ankle.

Montana opened up her dresser drawer and retrieved a semi-automatic weapon. She double-checked to make sure the safety was on and slipped it in her purse.

"Your car or mine?" Asia asked.

"Yours, because speed is of the essence."

Asia tried Mike again but he still didn't answer. Montana locked up and hopped in the passenger seat of Asia's sports car.

"Where are we going by the way?" she asked Asia.

"The outskirts of Dallas. Vanna's phone was tracked to this area on the other side of Mesquite."

"Off Highway 80?" Montana asked.

"Yes. Apparently, that's where her and Troy are being held."

"I hope they can get them out in time."

"Me too. Now buckle up because I'm not stopping for anyone."

Montana made sure her seatbelt was secure and held on for dear life as Asia made her way through traffic on Lyndon B. Johnson Freeway.

~ 6 ~

Sean used hand signals to his team so as to not alert the guards who were watching the fort. The fort looked like a huge compound surrounded by bob-wired fences with guards carrying assault rifles. Sean cut into one of the fences and made an entry way for him and his team. He snuck up on one of the guards, placed his arm around his neck, and twisted it. Sean didn't want him to make a loud thud so he carefully laid him down. This was part of the mission he didn't like. Killing never got easy. But it was either kill or be killed. Sean pointed toward the right as Mike followed suit with one of the other guards.

Normally, Sean would wait until nightfall to try to perform a rescue mission, but that luxury of time he didn't have. If he didn't get to Troy soon, he was afraid his brother-by-another-mother would be forever lost to him. Failure was not an option, as Sean blocked out any negative thinking and they continued to work their way outside of the view of the security cameras. He snatched up the walkie-talkie the guard had and continued to what appeared to be a huge warehouse.

Sean waited for Rex to pick the lock on the door. With another hand motion, Sean and his team made their way inside. Gunshots started ringing as soon as they entered. Sean barely missed being hit by one of the bullets.

"Hold them off," Sean yelled.

Sean tried not to shoot blindly but bullets were flying from everywhere. He searched each one of the small rooms that looked like cells, hoping he would find Troy or Savannah, but no such luck.

"The back. Just saw some go through the back," Mike yelled.

Sean caught a quick glimpse of a woman, who he assumed was Savannah, as she was pushed out the back door. Sean yelled, "Mike, we got to get to them before they get away."

Before he could get to the door, there was a loud explosion. Sean and Mike both fell back. Building fragments were everywhere. Sean cursed under his breath as he found strength and ran out the door.

A green Hummer jetted through the open field. He yelled in the small microphone clipped to his collar, "They are mobile. You guys head them off."

Fortunately for Sean, some of their men were waiting outside of the compound. Mike limped out behind Sean.

"Man, are you okay?" Sean asked.

"Go. I'll be all right," Mike assured him.

Sean was torn. He didn't want to leave Mike.

Mike shouted again, "Go."

Sean yelled, "I'll send one of the guys to pick you up in front. You don't want to walk too much on that leg."

Sean ran to the front and jumped in one of the cars. He didn't know who it belonged to but fortunately for him the keys were still in the ignition. He put the car in reverse and shifted the car in the direction of the Hummer. "Do you still have them in sight?" Sean asked Rex.

Rex responded, "Yes, but they are about to go head-on with this red sports car."

"Do whatever you can, but do not, and I repeat, do not let them out of your sight. I'm right behind y'all."

Sean pushed the gas pedal to the floor as the dirt behind him made a dust storm appear as he rushed through the wooded area. "Are they crazy?" Sean asked out loud as he saw the sports car and Hummer come so close to colliding.

The red sports car spun, missing the Hummer. Sean jumped on his brakes to avoid hitting it. The car he was in spun several times. When his car came to a complete stop, the engine cut off and then there's nothing.

"Sean." He heard a familiar voice call out his name.

To his surprise it was Montana and Asia. Several questions went through his mind, but he didn't have time to address them. He needed to get back behind Rex and that Hummer. "Asia, I hope you don't mind me driving your car. Hop in the back. Troy and Savannah were in that Hummer."

Asia didn't protest. Sean jumped behind the wheel and was soon back in pursuit. He called Rex. "Are you still on their tail?"

Rex didn't respond. "Rex, are you still on their tail?" he repeated. No response. Sean hit the steering wheel several times.

"Hey, watch it. This my car," Asia yelled.

The sight of the car Rex was driving wrapped around a tree shut Asia up. Montana yelled, "Oh, my God."

Sean jumped on the brakes and all of their bodies jerked forward. The Hummer was nowhere in sight. Sean hopped out of Asia's car and ran to the other vehicle. Rex's bloody body and the body of one of his other colleagues were in the front seat. He reached through the broken glass and checked each one of their pulses but felt nothing.

Mike pulled up in another car with some of their other men. Each was upset at the demise of the comrades.

"I don't know how I'm going to tell his mother," Sean said.

Sean didn't know when Montana had gotten out of the car, but she rubbed her hand on his back in a comforting manner.

"I'm sorry to hear about your friend."

Sean didn't mean to but he jerked back. "What are y'all doing here? This could have been you wrapped around the tree. I told you to stay at home."

Montana held her head in shame. Sean reached for her. "I'm sorry. I didn't mean to yell. But seriously, I didn't want to worry about you too."

"Savannah called us. We tried to reach Mike but we kept getting his voice mail." Montana looked at Mike who looked beat up and bruised. "Is he going to be okay?"

"He will be. I'm going to insist that he gets some medical treatment."

Asia was assisting Mike as he limped back to the other car.

Sean heard Montana say, "Asia, I'm going to stay with Sean. Go get Mike some medical help."

"Thanks, but you could have gone with them," Sean said.

"No. I'm not going to let you deal with this on your own."

Sean felt like he failed Troy and now Montana. The mission should have been simple. Now they were gone.

"I know my sister must really care about Mike because she left me the keys to her baby," Montana said, trying to lighten up the situation.

"Our cleanup crew will be here in a minute and then I can think about what my next move is going to be."

"If we would have known Savannah and Troy were in there, we wouldn't have moved," Montana said.

"No, you did the right thing. I just don't know if we'll have luck finding their location again."

"Well, maybe they left some clues back where they were being kept."

"You sure you haven't done these types of operations before?" Sean asked, knowing the answer that this wasn't something that Montana normally did, but he just wanted to see Montana's pretty smile. Her smile made him almost forget the issues that were staring him in the face.

I will find you and when I die, I'm going to deal with you personally. No interrogators," Sean snapped.

Montana wondered what he was talking to. He continued to say, "I had him on either one of their bodies is he did. Consider yourself a dead man," Sean ended the call. "If I didn't know better, I now know the man who has taken." They

~ 7 ~

Montana watched Sean direct his team as they eased the bodies of the dead men out of the car. They wanted to clean things up before the state troopers arrived on the scene. Montana wiped away a few tears as she saw the pain of loss in Sean's eyes. This was a simple diversion from her own problems. She closed her eyes and inhaled and exhaled.

Sean eased in Asia's driver's seat. "I got a team checking out the warehouse. We were this close to rescuing them."

Montana patted his right hand with her left. "You're doing your best. I know you are. I'm not upset with you."

"I'm glad you're not, because I am."

Sean's phone rang and without hesitating, he started talking to someone else, so Montana remained quiet. She didn't know who it was on the other end but she could hear Sean's end of the conversation.

"I will find you and when I do, I'm going to deal with you personally. No intercessors," Sean snapped.

Montana wondered who he was talking to.

He continued to say, "If one hair on either one of their bodies is harmed, consider yourself a dead man." Sean ended the call. "If I didn't know before, I now know for a fact who has them. They are now demanding money for their safe return."

Montana must have been holding her breath the whole time because she sighed. "How much?"

"Ten million."

Montana's mouth dropped. There was no way she would be able to come up with that much money. Tears started streaming down her face as she thought about the demise of Savannah.

Sean squeezed her hand. He was the one now comforting her. "I promise you I will get them back."

"If I lose Savannah, I don't know if I can go on." Montana's lips shivered as she talked.

"I'm going to have you drop me off at my place so I can get cleaned up and go tell Rex's mother about her son."

"I'm being so selfish. I'm sorry."

"No. You're very calm under the circumstances. I commend you for that."

"Why don't you get cleaned up and I'll wait on you and go with you to tell his mom. Maybe seeing a woman with you will help ease the situation."

"I'll think about it."

An hour later, Montana and Sean were knocking on the door of Rex's mother. The quaint, small house had a beautiful arrangement of colorful flowers adorning the lawn.

"Sean, it's been a long time." Rex's mother had aged gracefully. Her salt and pepper gray hair was pulled back in a bun and she didn't have many wrinkles. "And you've brought your girlfriend with you."

"I'm not . . ." Montana started to say, but caught herself.

"Come on in, you two, and have a seat." She placed one of her hands in the pocket of her pink floral house dress.

Montana remained quiet and followed Sean and Rex's mother into her living room. The sofa still had the plastic on it. Montana took a seat next to Sean.

"Mrs. Titus, I don't know how to say this."

Mrs. Titus removed a handkerchief from her housecoat pocket. "He's gone isn't he?"

Sean shook his head up and down. "It was instant. He didn't suffer."

"I knew this day was coming. Just hoped I would be old and senile by then." She attempted to laugh as the tears started streaming down her face.

Montana got up to comfort her. "If there's anything I can do, let me know."

Mrs. Titus said, "Can you hand me the phone off the table?"

Montana looked up in the direction she was looking, went and retrieved the cordless phone, and handed it to her.

"I'm going to walk you two out first." She stood up while gripping the phone.

Montana looked at Sean and pleaded with her eyes not to leave. Sean said, "We'll remain here until you can get someone else here."

"I'm okay, honey. I'm going to make a few calls and take this time by myself to reflect on some things. You know once I call and tell everyone I'm not going to get a moment of peace."

"But—" Montana said.

"No buts. Dear, you're a sweetheart. Sean, you're lucky to have this woman." Mrs. Titus took Montana's hand and placed it in Sean's. She said, "Now you two run along. Sean, have his body sent to Ledbetter Funeral Home."

Sean and Montana hugged her on their way out the door.

"Are you sure it's okay to leave her by herself?" Montana asked as they walked to Sean's car.

"She's taking it better than I thought she would."

"My baby." Mrs. Titus's loud wail could be heard from where they stood.

Montana's heart ached for her. One of the neighbors walked to the fence. "I just heard her scream. What's going on?"

Sean asked, "Are you close to her?"

"Yes, Betty and I have been friends for over thirty years."

"She's going to need you. Rex was killed today."

"Oh my God. Betty, I'm coming," the elderly woman cried out.

Sean and Montana sat in the car until they saw the elderly woman enter Mrs. Titus's home. Silence filled the car.

~ 8 ~

Sean didn't have time to deal with Rex's death right now. He had to figure out a way to avoid any more deaths. Guilt tugged at him as he tried to play back what he could have done better so that Rex could still be alive.

Montana said, "There's nothing you could have done. It was an accident. As fast as they were going, the car must have skidded when they went around that curve."

Sean knew Montana was right but it didn't stop him from feeling guilty. He was determined, now more than ever, to find Troy. He couldn't let Rex's death be in vain.

Sean glanced at Montana who was, now, on her cell phone. The compassion she showed Rex's mom touched him deeply. He was not one to believe in love at first sight, but he could actually say he knew he fell in love with Montana the day he laid eyes on her.

The problem lay in the fact that he was not sure it was possible for her to reciprocate that love. The same compassion she showed Rex's mom she had displayed to him, so he knew it was just in her nature. That he was no one special was his life's greatest fear. No one would ever feel that he was special. His mom abandoned him when he was a baby and if it hadn't been for his maternal grandmother and grandfather, he would have been a ward of the state. Sean never knew his dad. Major, Montana's daddy, seemed to take on the father image in his life when he joined the military. He hoped one day, when things were back to normal—as normal as could be with his job—that Montana would see him as someone special and give him the opportunity to show her how special she was to him.

"That was Asia. Mike's okay. They wanted to keep him overnight for observation, but you know how stubborn he can be."

"From what I hear, your sister can be pretty stubborn too."

"That we both can agree on." Montana chuckled.

Sean drove to his place and pulled up beside Asia's car. "Montana, thanks for going with me. I really appreciate it."

"There's no way I would let you go by yourself."

Montana clicked the alarm off and stood by Asia's car.

Sean's phone buzzed. He read the text. "Look. I got to get to the office. I'll call you."

"Is it about my sister?" Montana asked.

"Yes."

"Then I'm coming with you," she responded.

Sean didn't have time to go back and forth with Montana. "Come on."

Montana hit the alarm button on her keychain. She got back in the car with Sean and he pulled off.

Boom! The sound startled them both. They looked up and Asia's car blew up into little pieces.

Montana's hand couldn't stop shaking. "If I didn't come with you, I would be dead."

Sean called the office. After telling them what just happened, he said, "Have the squad come scan for any more devices." He gave out some instructions and then addressed Montana. "Whoever set the bomb up in the car assumed that it was my car."

"What if Asia or I would have driven the car? We would have been blown to pieces."

"I got two hours to figure out our next move. We will not be giving them ten million dollars."

Montana wasn't paying Sean any attention. Her ear was glued to her phone. "Bad news, Asia. Is your insurance up to date?"

Sean couldn't hear Asia's response. Montana said from her end, "I don't know if someone bombing your car is part of your policy plan but I hope so because your car just blew up."

Asia's voice got louder because Sean could hear her from the driver's seat.

"It's at Sean's place. His team is headed over. Police report. Hmm. I don't know." Montana addressed Sean. "Can she get a police report for her insurance company?"

"I'll make sure she gets one," Sean responded. Sean called one of his employees. "Make sure there's an official filing so the owner of the car can file her insurance."

Sean was used to multitasking but it was becoming difficult to concentrate as he drove away toward the office. He tried to figure out what his next move would be, and he wondered what was on Montana's mind.

Montana remained quiet the rest of the ride into the office located on the outskirts of Dallas. From outward appearances, it looked like any other office building. Sean gave the password to the guard at the gate. "This is Red. She'll be our guest."

Montana spoke for the first time since getting off the phone with Asia. "I haven't heard that code name since you guys trained me."

"I know. You actually turn red when you're excited or upset," Sean said. He wished he could have taken it back. He didn't want Montana to know he had paid that much attention to her.

"Asia's upset at me about her car. But I know she's just taking out her frustrations on me because of Savannah's situation."

"I guess it's times like these I'm glad to be an only child."

"Being an only child I'm sure has its perks, but I wouldn't trade my sisters in for all the money in the world." Sadness filled Montana's eyes.

Sean would do whatever he needed to do to replace that look in her eyes. Sean found a parking spot in the covered parking area. Confident they were now safe and secure since they were on Sean's turf, Sean held Montana's door open and she followed him to the elevator. He entered a code and they stepped into the elevator. When they made it to the basement, there were about ten other people in the room.

"Everybody, this is Red. She's here because her sister is the one abducted with Troy. She's also here because, as you can tell, she was able to transform my look, and just in case we need to send some people in, she can assist in doing that." Sean hadn't asked Montana if she would do it and he hated putting her on the spot, but he needed to get her involved somehow so she could feel useful in the dire situation.

A woman in her early twenties entered and handed each person, excluding Montana, a manila folder. Sean opened it up and glanced through it. Inside were pictures of Troy and Savannah being placed in the Hummer. The folder also had pictures and a long bio on each assailant, including the dead ones.

Sean skimmed through the information before addressing his team. "We need to handle this like any other abduction so that we won't make any more mistakes. We've lost two comrades. Jimmy, thanks for letting Harold's parents know. I don't think I could have handled doing both right now."

Jimmy shook his head. He said, "I got several cases of money ready to make the exchange."

"We're not giving them ten million dollars. If we do that, they are as good as dead," Sean said. Sean did his best not to look in Montana's direction. The way she tilted her head and licked her lips had him thinking erotic thoughts instead of what he should have been concentrating on.

Jimmy said, "But I got it together just in case."

Sean looked back at them all. "Giving them that money is the last resort. Does anyone disagree with me?"

Mumblings were heard but everyone agreed with Sean.

"How y'all going to have a meeting without me?" Mike said after bursting in the room with Asia fast on his heels.

"Sis, we need to talk," Asia mouthed to Montana.

Sean noticed. He said to Montana, "There's a room next door if you two need to talk." He looked back at his comrades. "Someone get Mike a seat. Where was I?"

Sean continued going through the profiles as Montana and Asia left the room.

tapped her toe. She looked at Asia. "Don't worry, they'll right yourself."

After going back and forth with the representative many minutes, Montana got off the phone. "Your check should be ready by the end of the week."

Asia cried, "I can't believe I'm so emotional over this."

~ 9 ~

Montana would have rather stayed with Sean so she could stay abreast on what was going on, but instead she followed Asia to the next room. "Do you know the insurance rep told me they might not pay? They said it's a special circumstance and my policy might not cover it."

Montana tuned Asia out as she ranted on and on about the insurance company. Montana's mind was in the next room. She needed to know what Sean was planning next.

Asia pouted, "I don't know how much more of this I can take."

"Give me your phone," Montana said. "What's their number?"

"It's the last one dialed," Asia said as she handed Montana her purple diamond-studded phone.

"I need to speak with a supervisor," Montana said as soon as someone answered. "I don't care. I need to speak with a supervisor." Montana tapped her foot. She looked at Asia. "Don't worry. They will replace your car."

After going back and forth with the supervisor for fifteen minutes, Montana got off the phone. "Your check should be ready by the end of the week."

Asia cried. "I can't believe I'm so emotional over this."

Montana wrapped her arms around her. "Sis, it's going to be okay."

"Here I am worried about replacing a car. If something happens to Vanna, she can't be replaced," Asia managed to say in between sobs.

Montana dried the tears that threatened to fall from her eyes. Asia was the baby of the family and she sometimes forgot that. They normally sparred and, admittedly, over some silly things. Right now, Savannah wasn't around to break the squabbles up. Montana would be more careful so as not to give Asia a hard time. She didn't realize how fragile Asia was right now. She rocked her sister in her arms until Asia pulled away.

Asia wiped her face with the back of her hand. "Look at me, crying like a little girl."

"It's okay. This has been a stressful day." Montana tried to make light of the situation.

"Mike said that the people who have Savannah won't do anything to her as long as Sean cooperates."

"I don't know if Mike told you, but they want ten million dollars. Sean doesn't want to give them the money."

Asia stormed out of the room. Montana tried to stop her but to no avail. Asia stormed into the room where everybody else was. "If you have it, you need to give it to them. That's my sister's life you're playing with."

Montana said, "I tried to explain to her why."

Mike stood up. "Asia, let us handle this. We're the experts."

"Well, if you were such an expert, you would have rescued her and we wouldn't be having this conversation, now would we?" Asia took her stance with folded arms and pouted.

Sean addressed the group. "We're through here. Waiting on the call at eighteen hundred. Everybody be prepared to move at that time."

Everyone left the room except for Mike, Asia, Sean, and Montana. Montana said, "Asia, Sean knows what he's doing."

"Oh, so now you're on his side. It was you who wanted the police to handle it in the first place."

"I know, but I was wrong. Let Sean and Mike do their jobs."

Asia plopped down in one of the chairs. "I need to know everything you have planned, and I do mean everything, or else I'm calling the police."

Montana looked at Sean. "She's serious, so I suggest you comply."

Sean held a chair out. "Have a seat."

Montana took a seat. Sean remained standing. He handed Montana and Asia each a manila folder.

Sean said, "These are the people who we know have Troy and Savannah."

"I'm reading this, but who are these people? Why are they targeting you?" Montana asked.

"One of our comrades went undercover and became a part of their elite group. They are dangerous men and women whose sole purpose is to destroy the government by any means necessary," Mike said.

Sean interjected, "I was on the team instrumental in taking out one of their leaders. I also ended up killing a few people, and one happened to be the son of the head leader of this organization. Until this happened, I thought my identity was unknown, but I underestimated them."

"But did they have to take Savannah?" Asia asked.

"It's fortunate for Savannah that she's still alive, because groups like this normally take their intended victim and kill everyone else."

Montana sighed. "Thanks. I guess we should be happy about that."

"So, what's next? Why not give them the money?" Asia stared at Sean.

"If we give them the money they will kill Troy and Savannah. If we don't give it to them, we will buy ourselves some time."

Mike said, "We tried to track Savannah's phone and we were able to but we lost track."

"Her battery probably went out," Montana said.

"Exactly, so we do know they are now north of Dallas. Our sources tell us there's an area of land north of McKinney that this group is known to use so we got people checking it out now. This time, when we make our move, they will not see us coming." Sean did his best to assure Montana.

"I heard you mention eighteen hundred. So at six o'clock the drop is supposed to take place?"

"No, at six I will get further instructions. Everyone just needs to be prepared to make a move just in case. We got everybody on this." Sean's eyes seemed to pierce right through Montana.

"What can me and Asia do? This waiting is really getting to us."

"Try staying out of our way," Mike said.

Asia rolled her eyes. "You're lucky you're already hurt, or I would . . ."

"Or you would what?" Mike dared her.

"Never mind," Asia responded.

"Hmm. That's a first. Asia backing down to you. Is there something you two aren't telling me?" Montana asked as she looked back and forth between Mike and Asia.

"There's nothing to tell," Asia said.

"You got that right," Mike responded.

"Well, while you two are trying to figure out your relationship, Red, I need you to come with me."

Montana eyed Asia and Mike, but followed Sean out of the room and down the hall to another office. As soon as the doors were closed, Sean pulled her into his arms and planted a long, juicy kiss on her.

Sean exhaled. "Now, I can concentrate." Sean walked to his desk and picked up the phone.

Montana's hand lightly brushed her lips where Sean's lips had just been. She asked herself, *What just happened here?* She didn't have time to dwell on it, because Sean said, "Come on. We got a solid lead."

Montana pushed the thoughts of the kiss out of her mind and followed him.

~ 10 ~

By the time Sean made it to the garage, his ten-man team was in place. Sean, Montana, Asia, and Mike rode in one black SUV, while others piled into the remaining vehicles. Each was fully loaded with weapons.

Sean jumped on Central Expressway and headed north. The convoy of cars was right behind him. He took a quick glance at Montana. "We need you and Asia to stay in the car. Only reason why I'm allowing you to come is so that we won't have an incident like the last time."

"Don't worry. We can handle ourselves," Montana said as she pulled out her small hand-gun.

"Glad to see you're packing. Let's just hope you won't have to use it. But, if you do, aim to kill," Sean said. His cell phone rang. He hit the speaker button.

"Patterson, you got our money?" a computer-generated voice asked from the other end.

"When you can stop hiding behind an electronic device, then we can talk."

A sinister laugh filled the car from the phone. "The clock is ticking. Small bills, please, and they better not be marked."

"How do I know they are still alive?" Sean asked.

"You have to trust me." The sinister laugh started back up.

"Send me a picture to my phone of both parties and then maybe we can negotiate." Sean hit the end button. He handed Mike his phone.

Ten minutes later, Mike checked the text messages. "They sent them. Troy's beat up badly but Savannah looks fine under the circumstances. She looks tired but that's it."

"Are they together or separate?"

The picture showed a battered Troy sitting on a hard concrete floor in one room and Savannah was tied up to a chair in aother small room. She wasn't bruised but her eyes looked weary.

"Looks like they are keeping them in two different rooms," Mike responded.

"Send them to Chad," Sean directed.

Sean's phone rang. Mike hit the speaker button.

"Are you satisfied?" the mysterious caller asked.

"I need time to come up with that type of money," Sean responded, although he didn't have any intention of giving them the $10 million they requested.

"I will give you twenty-four hours. If you don't have it, the deal is off. You'll have two lives on your head." The caller hung up.

"So, are you giving them the money?" Montana asked.

"Not if I can help it," Sean assured her. Sean took the next exit.

"This isn't McKinney," Asia said.

"We need to wait until nightfall. In the meantime, I'll go get us some rooms." Sean pulled up in front of the hotel. "Come on, Montana. I need you."

Sean held the back door open. Montana eased her five-eight, medium frame out the vehicle. He reached for her hand. She didn't resist.

"So are we newlyweds, or an old married couple?" Montana jokingly asked.

"Let's be newlyweds because that comes with benefits."

"Don't even go there. You gets none of this."

"One day I will. Mark my words," Sean said as the automatic door of the hotel opened.

The eager hotel clerk took his credit card and gave him the room keys. "You can get to your room through the side door down that hall. Just park on the side."

Sean was happy about that. "Dear, I'll bring the car around. Just meet me at the side door."

Montana took one of the room keys and walked away toward the hallway. Sean walked back out and alerted the team to follow him. There weren't too many parking places on the side so four of the cars had to park in other areas.

Sean waited until everybody was at the doorway and they all entered at the same time. All twelve of them convened in the hotel suite.

"I'm going to order pizza and drinks. Anybody feels the need to take a nap, now is the time. We need to be in our positions by twenty-three hundred," Sean said.

Asia yawned. "I can't believe all of this has happened in less than twenty-four hours. I feel like I've run a marathon."

"Me too," Montana added.

"Ladies, you two can have the bedroom to relax and us guys will stay out here," Sean said.

"That's so generous of you." Montana flashed a quick smile. "Sean, can I talk to you in private?"

Sean followed Montana to the bedroom. She closed the door. "I would have gotten them another room if I knew you wanted to consummate our fake marriage." Sean couldn't resist teasing her.

"You got jokes. I just wanted you to know that I appreciate all that you're doing. I know this hasn't been easy on you. Forgive Asia and me for some of our actions, but I do trust that you'll get my sister back safely."

Sean reached for Montana. "Come here."

Surprisingly, Montana allowed him to embrace her. Montana's head fell on his chest. Sean thought this was better than sex. Having Montana in his arms and this close after nights of dreaming of her was a dream come true.

Montana gently pushed away. "I didn't mean to get so mushy. Wake me up when the pizza comes. I think I'm going to take you up on that offer and take a nap. This has been a very trying day."

Sean left to give Montana peace. Asia wouldn't let Mike out of her sight. Sean retrieved several twenties out of his pocket and handed them to one of his workers. "Here's the money for the pizza. I'll be in the room if anyone needs me. I need to think."

"I hope that's all you're doing," Asia said.

"Montana's sleeping," Sean assured her.

"Um huh," Asia responded.

Mike said, "Asia, get out of their business."

Sean listened to Mike and Asia's back-and-forth banter as he picked up his laptop from the table and headed to the bedroom.

He watched Montana's chest rise up and fall down as she slept. It took all of his control not to go lie down in the bed beside her. Instead, he placed the laptop down on the nearby table, and reached for the bedspread and pulled it up until it reached her shoulders. She looked to be at peace but he knew she wasn't.

Sean sat in the chair and turned his computer on. He studied the photos he had of the compound on the other side of McKinney. He went over the plans he and his team had discussed to make sure there were no loopholes. They couldn't afford any because if they moved again, they might not be able to track them down and that would be the demise of Troy and Savannah.

~ 11 ~

Montana blinked her eyes a few times. She felt disoriented. It took her a moment or two to realize she wasn't at home but in a strange hotel. His back was to her, but she could see Sean's head nod off.

She slipped out of the bed and tapped him on the shoulder.

"You're up," Sean said in between yawns.

"I think you need to take a nap. You were asleep at the computer."

"I'm fine. I just dozed off."

Montana reached for his hand and he allowed her to pull him up, and followed her to the bed. "Lie down."

"I don't have time."

"One hour. Give yourself one hour and I promise you, you'll be rejuvenated. Me, I dozed off for, what, about fifteen minutes and I feel a little better already."

"Twenty minutes," Sean responded.

"I'll be sure no one disturbs you."

Sean sat on the bed. "You're going to be my bodyguard."

"And a good one at that," Montana responded.

Sean placed his hands behind his head and lay on the pillow.

Montana lay next to him.

They both were awakened when they heard a knock at the door.

"Come in," Montana responded as she sat up.

Asia peeped in with a pizza box. "The pizza finally arrived. Had to call because it took them an entire hour to get here."

Sean was the first to speak. "Lay it on the table. I'm not really hungry."

"Well, you need to eat something," Montana said.

Sean looked at Asia. "Is she always like this?"

"Yes. So I suggest you do what she says or she will nag you to death."

Montana rolled her eyes. "I'm going to the bathroom. You two can keep talking about me like I'm not in the room."

Montana left the bedroom. The men looked at her funny. She didn't realize why until she saw her reflection in the bathroom mirror. Her hair was in disarray. *If anyone didn't know better, they probably think me and Sean . . . No,*

they wouldn't think that. Why wouldn't they?
Montana was so embarrassed.

She used her hand and pulled her hair together
and redid her ponytail. Now she looked present-
able. She did her best to hold her head up high
and reentered the main area of the room. Instead
of going back to the bedroom, she took a seat near
Mike.

"So, are you feeling better?" she asked.

"I would be feeling great if your sister wouldn't
insist that I take these meds. I have to be alert
and they make me drowsy," he responded.

Montana said, "You must be a glutton for
pain."

"No, but I need to be alert for what's about to
take place."

"Compromise. Take half of a pill. That'll still
help ease some of the pain."

Mike appeared to be thinking about it. "Can
you pass me a slice of pizza and a Coke?"

"Water would be better," Montana said.

"Coke would be fine," Mike responded.

"You and Sean can be so stubborn."

"It's a man thing." Mike laughed.

Montana didn't. After she cut the pill in half
and handed it to Mike and she saw him swallow
it, she got up and went back to the bedroom.
Asia's and Sean's backs were toward the door

and they were engrossed in whatever was on his laptop screen.

Montana cleared her throat. "Good thing I came back to join the party," Montana said.

"Sis, he was just showing me the pictures from inside the compound. Based on the pictures sent to his cell phone, he knows exactly which room Savannah is in."

Sean interjected, "She's kept in a room near the back, so some of us will attack from that end."

"What about Troy?" Montana asked.

"He's in the middle and will be harder to get to."

Sean must have noticed the frown that swept across Montana's face because he continued, to say, "Don't worry. It'll be challenging but it's not impossible."

Montana sighed. "I'll just be glad when all of this is over with."

Sean stood up. "Well, rest up, ladies. We'll be headed out shortly." He left Asia and Montana alone.

As soon as the door closed, Asia blurted out, "He's crazy about you."

"Excuse me," Montana responded, as she sat on the bed and crossed her legs.

Asia and Montana sat around doing their best to keep their mind off the danger Savannah was in. Montana picked up the remote control to turn up the volume on the television with hopes of tuning out Asia.

"Don't you see how his eyes light up every time you enter the room?"

"No. I don't pay him that much attention." Montana turned the volume back down since it was obvious Asia wasn't going to stop talking.

"Whatever. I see how you be checking him out on the sly." Asia took a seat on the bed next to her.

"Okay, he's fine, but he's in the wrong occupation for me. I want a man with a nine-to-five job. Not one who gets off on adventures. I hated worrying about whether or not our dad would make it back home safely. I don't know if I could deal with my man doing what our father did.

"You're so boring at times," Asia said.

"You're one to talk." Montana felt an attitude coming on.

"You are. You've always tried to play things by the book. Look what that got you. You're almost thirty. Single and alone."

"But I'm not lonely and I'm not desperate for a man," Montana responded.

"Still. I think you should give Sean a chance."

"He hasn't made a pass at me," Montana lied. She failed to admit the two kisses they'd shared.

Sean flipped his car lights off. The other vehicles in the convoy did the same. The cars parked in an open field not too far from the road. "Ladies, shoot first and don't worry about asking questions if anyone besides one of us approaches this vehicle," Sean said as he unbuckled his seatbelt.

Montana gripped her handgun.

"I'm going to be in the other car watching the monitors that we've tapped into," Mike said as he exited the door as soon as it came to a standstill.

"The compound is about a mile ahead. Be prepared for anything. The radio is here so you can keep up with what's going on. Try not to be alarmed by the sounds you might hear." Sean knew that there would be some bullets flying and possibly bloodshed so he didn't want them to be freaked out about it.

"Just bring my sister out," Montana said as their eyes locked.

Sean broke the trance and eased out of the car. He and the rest of the team were dressed in army fatigues. Their faces were now all covered with paint so they could blend in with the surroundings. All eight of the men were in top physical condition and had been on many rescue missions. They just hated being on one that involved rescuing one of their own. They were all heavily armed with assault rifles, hand grenades and other artillery they may need to make the rescue a successful operation, as they made their way silently through the wooded area. Sean's sources had given them all the information they needed to do the rescue mission.

"Mike, we're almost there. Do you have control of their cameras?"

"Give me about five and I will," Mike responded.

Sean's heart rate increased. It seemed as if the sound of his beating heart was getting louder and louder as he and his team waited for Mike to give them the word that the security system and security cameras had been deactivated. Mike was a master behind the computer and could infiltrate any security system. They stood outside of the wired ten-foot fence.

"Set," Mike responded. "I was able to deactivate the security system and cameras for ten minutes. I'll try to make it fifteen."

"Rock and roll," Sean said barely above a whisper.

Jason used the wire cutters to get through the fence. He motioned for them to crawl through. They did, one at a time. Sean was the first one to go through as he scouted the area. Everyone listened to Mike in their earpieces as he informed them of the location of the guards.

Sean snuck up behind one, twisted his neck and he immediately died. Jason and the other guys got the other three guards and killed them without any retaliation.

Mike's voice rang in his ear. "Eight minutes."

Sean held up his hand. He used his fingers to count down. One finger came out, then two, and when the third finger extended, they all scattered toward the building. Sean peaked through the windows as they walked outside of the warehouse. He held his hand up in a ball to indicate he'd located one of the captives. Savannah's head was drooped over so he hoped she was okay. He held one finger up to indicate that there was one person guarding.

Mike said in his ear, "You have a better chance going through the back. No one's there."

Sean pointed to his right. He eased past his men.

Mike gave out instructions. "Jason, need you to stay near the window where Savannah is. Douglas and Ray, make sure you cover the other side. Everybody else, you know what to do."

Sean pulled out some tools from his waistband. He eased the window off. After making sure the coast was clear, he climbed through, followed by four other team members.

Mike said in the earpiece, "I haven't been able to locate Troy. The cameras have scanned each room."

Sean stuck the mirror out in the hallway to double-check to see if anyone was there. The hallway was empty. He eased down the hallway toward the place Troy was originally supposed to be. The room was empty.

"Coming your way at six o'clock angle," Mike said.

Sean ducked back in the room, barely missing being detected. When Mike informed him the coast was clear, he eased back in the hallway. He headed toward the room where Savannah was being held prisoner.

Mike told him the guard wasn't budging from his spot near the door. Sean pulled a red-tipped dart from his waistband and knocked on the door, easing to the side of it. The guard opened the door. Sean threw the dart and it struck the other man in the side of his neck. Sean rushed up and caught him before he dropped to the floor.

Savannah was tied and bound and had a scared look in her eyes.

"It's okay, I'm here to rescue you. I work with Troy, remember?"

Savannah shook her head up and down as Sean untied her hands and her legs. He removed the gag over her mouth.

She started coughing. "There's a bomb under my chair. If I move, it'll explode."

Mike's voice sounded through his earpiece. "Four minutes."

Sean clicked a button on his waist. "We got a problem. There's a bomb under her chair. I'm going to have to deactivate it."

Sweat started pouring down Savannah's face. "Tell my sisters I love them."

Sean responded, "I need you to stay calm. You're going to be able to tell them yourself. So don't freak out on me."

"I'm worried about Troy. They keep telling me that he's dead."

"He's alive."

"You're not just telling me that are you?" Savannah asked in a weak breath.

"I need you to be my lookout. I locked the door, but let me know if you see the doorknob move while I'm concentrating on deactivating this bomb."

Mike said, "Three minutes. Troy's been located."

"Good news. Troy's been located," Sean said as he slid on his back under the chair. He said a prayer and used the small wire cutters and clipped the wires in order of color. "One more and then you're free."

"Hurry up because I have to pee," Savannah said.

"I'm not R. Kelly so I don't want you to pee on me so I better hurry," Sean jokingly said to ease the tension.

He clicked the red wire and closed his eyes hoping his memory of disarming this type of bomb was correct.

"One minute," Mike said.

Sean said, "We don't have time to go out the way I came in."

Sean opened the window and helped Savannah out, while Jason kept her from falling on the ground. "Let's go."

Mike repeated it in his ear so the entire team could hear. "Time's up."

Sean said, "Savannah, I know you might be a little weak, but I need you to run as fast as you can. Don't look back. Follow Jason. I'm right behind you."

"Where's Troy?"Savannah asked.

"Troy will be fine. I got other men looking for him," Sean responded.

Even in the dark, Sean could see Savannah's fear, but time was no longer on their side. They jetted through the field. Gunshots were heard from behind them. The men with Sean fired back shooting and killing some of the men after them.

Savannah wasn't a track star but was physically fit so she ran fast enough to keep up with Jason. Sean looked back just in time to see part of the building blow up. He hoped and prayed the rest of his team were able to get out before the explosion and he hoped Troy was with them.

"Mike, we're a half mile away."

Mike said, "I'm sending Asia with the car. My foot's swollen."

"Tell her to keep the lights off. Meet her on the road," Sean responded. "There's a car coming for us. We need to meet them on the road, but we might have company so let's stay along the edges of the trees."

Savannah responded, "Okay. " She started coughing.

"Are you okay?" Sean asked.

"Just thirsty but other than that I'm fine," she responded, as they continued along the path.

Before Sean could blink, Asia had pulled the SUV near them. Sean jumped out to flag her down to let her know their location. She jumped on the brakes, barely missing Sean.

"Scoot over," he said as he swung the driver's side door open.

Asia did as instructed. Jason opened the passenger door and helped Savannah in before getting in behind her.

"Vanna, it's you," Asia screamed.

Sean saw in his rearview mirror Montana and Savannah hug. The sisters' reunion was short-lived because out of nowhere bullets started flying.

Sean quickly turned the SUV around and gassed it. "Mike, we got company. Saddle up."

"I'm already on it."

Sean said, "Everybody buckle up . . . This is going to be a bumpy ride."

~ 13 ~

Montana held on to Savannah as Sean sped down the roadway. Tears stained her face. It all seemed surreal. "You sure you're okay?" Montana asked over and over.

"I'm fine. Thirsty, but I'm fine."

Jason reached into the back of the SUV and handed her a bottle of water.

Savannah gulped it down as if she hadn't had anything to drink in days. Savannah was the older sister but, right now, she needed to be nurtured. Montana held Savannah's hand to comfort her and so that they both would know this wasn't a dream. Savannah was free and had been reunited with her family.

Montana said a silent prayer of thanks to God. She looked back to see if the car was still behind them. It appeared that Sean had lost them, but that's when she noticed the car speed past an eighteen-wheeler. What she saw extended from the car scared her.

"Oh my God. Looks like they have a missile," she screamed.

"Hold on."

"Hold on? You save Vanna just for us all to get blown up?" Asia shouted from the front seat.

"Calm down, Asia. Sean knows what he's doing," Montana said in Sean's defense.

When Sean said he was going to gun it, he meant it. He went so fast that everybody's backs were glued to the seats. He took an exit near Plano. Even at night, traffic was heavy on the popular road. "Out now," Sean said as he zipped the vehicle behind a building.

Everybody jumped out and ran behind Sean as they went into a residential neighborhood.

"I have a friend who stays on the next street. We just need to make it there in one piece," Jason said.

"Call him and let him know to expect us," Sean ordered.

Savannah stopped and started coughing. "I'm okay. Just a little weak," she said.

Sean threw Savannah up around his shoulders and they ran behind Jason.

Jason's friend didn't seem to be fazed by the sight of them as they quickly entered what looked like a normal one-story brick suburban home.

But once they entered, Montana realized there wasn't anything normal behind the doors. It looked like she had stepped into an army barrack with all of the arsenal she saw sprawled across the table where they were now.

"Sean, heard good things about you," the stranger with the long white beard said.

"Mack. You're a legend."

"And the good thing is I've lived through it," Mack stated nonchalantly.

Sean said, "Thanks for letting us camp out here until we can regroup."

"Man, I haven't had this much excitement since my wife told me she was leaving me."

Montana asked, "I hate to bother you, but do you have a bathroom?"

"Pretty lady, I have anything you want. It's down the hall to the right."

"Thank you, sir."

"Sir. You hear that, Jason? She's out of my league, man."

"You'll have to fight Sean for her," Jason responded.

The sisters walked to the bathroom. Montana noticed the sad look on Savannah's face.

"Vanna, everything will be okay. Sean is doing everything he can." Montana said

"No one has said anything about Troy. Where is Troy is all I want to know," Savannah said.

"Asia, finish helping her get cleaned up. I'll go check with Sean and see what's going on."

Montana eased back in the room and remained quiet as she listened from the doorway to Sean and Jason talking.

"Have a seat," Sean said without once looking in her direction.

She should have known he knew she was there. She did as instructed and continued to listen.

Sean said, "Mike said a few of our men are hurt and one is missing."

"Troy? What about Troy?" Montana blurted out.

"We didn't get him," Sean said disappointedly.

"What am I going to tell Vanna?"

"Tell me what?" she asked as she walked back in the living room area with Asia.

Montana patted the seat next to her. Savannah took a seat. "They were not able to get to Troy."

Savannah wailed. "No, please not Troy. Sean, tell me she's wrong."

Sean confirmed what Montana said. "We weren't able to get to him. We tried."

"Nooo." Savannah's voice trailed off as Montana rocked her back and forth in her arms.

Sean's phone rang. He answered and then said, "Our rides are here."

He thanked the old guy for his hospitality and they exited. Two SUVs were waiting for them.

"Ladies, I'm going to have the driver take you to a safe house until we can be sure that your homes are safe."

"I don't have anything to wear. I'm tired, sweaty, and sticky," Asia complained.

Mike said, "There's some clothes there. Might not be the exact sizes you all wear, but they'll do. We would rather be safe than have something happen to you ladies."

Montana agreed. "Right. Come on, Asia."

Sean held the door open as Asia and Savannah eased in the back seat of the SUV. Sean hugged Montana tight and whispered in her ear, "Everything is going to be okay. I'll call you."

Sean kissed Montana quickly on the lips right before she eased in her seat next to Savannah. He shut the door. Montana's hand grazed her lips. She pushed her feelings for Sean to the backburner. She placed her hand on top of Savannah's and squeezed it. She would do her best to comfort Savannah as she dealt with the possibility of having lost Troy.

~ 14 ~

Sean was running on pure adrenaline. He took the moment of being in the passenger seat to exhale. They were headed to the office so the team could debrief. With the way things were going, they would have to figure out their next move. Troy's abductors would be upset and there was no telling how they would retaliate.

"Mike, you're looking a little pale, man," Sean said.

"I'll be all right," Mike responded.

Mike, Sean, and Jason heard loud talking as they walked toward the conference room. "What is going on?" Sean asked as he opened the door to the conference room.

"Sean, I've been waiting for you," a familiar voice said.

The crowd of people moved away. The sight of Troy, bruised and in torn clothing, was a sigh of relief. Sean didn't expect to get so emotional, but he was just happy to see his friend, his brother, safe and back among them.

He rushed over to him and they gave each other a brotherly hug. "Man, we thought they had got you."

Troy patted Victor on the back. "Your man here got me out."

"Vic, we thought you were a goner. Man, why didn't you radio in?"

"I dropped my radio. I was about to go back for it when the explosion happened," Victor responded.

He looked at Troy. "Man, you just don't know how happy I am to see you. What happened? Somebody get this man a seat and a drink."

"I'm all right," Troy said as he took a seat in one of the brown leather chairs.

"Victor, did you get our main target?" Sean asked.

"No, he got away, but I did kill his sidekick."

Troy said, "We don't have much time. They are plotting something and whatever it is, it'll affect everybody in the DFW area. They want to send a message to the rest of the country."

"Do you know when this is supposed to happen?" Before Sean could get his answer his cell phone rang. "Quiet, everybody."

Sean put the phone on speaker.

"I guess I'll have to figure out another way for you to give me that ten million dollars," Troy and Savannah's kidnapper said.

"We got what we wanted so we have nothing else to talk about," Sean said.

"If you hang up the phone, the lives of a million people will be in jeopardy."

Mike used the computer to see if he could trace the call. Sean said, "What do you want? Ten million today. Five million tomorrow. What do you want to go away and forget whatever is going through your sick mind?"

"We are not going away. The government tried to get rid of us, but we're still standing. I want what's rightfully mine," the man on the other end said.

"And that's what?"

"Freedom. Freedom from taxes and to live my life without the government always in my business."

"Why don't you just move to another country and you wouldn't have to worry about it?" Sean asked.

"You can stop trying to track me. As you can tell, I'm hard to catch up with."

Mike shook his head to indicate no luck in tracing it.

Sean said, "Again, move if you don't like it here."

"My forefathers helped build this country and I will not be run from my birthright."

Sean knew there was no rationalizing with an irrational-minded person. Driskoll was definitely not a normal person. "Norman . . . I can call you Norman?"

"As long as I can call you Sean."

"Well, now that we're on a first-name basis, tell me, Norman, what will the ten million dollars guarantee?"

"Since you have your friend and his girlfriend back, I think I want more than that. Let's see, how much do you think it's worth to save DFW?"

"I don't have time to play this game with you. Call me back when you have something to say."

There was a pause. Then the guy known as Norman yelled, "Do you think this is a game? Do you remember what happened in 2009? Were we playing? Do you want to see the same thing happen here? It's up to you, Sean."

Sean's mind flashed back to four years ago. The memory of that organization going on a killing spree lingered in his mind. They targeted all of the mayors within the state of Arizona. It was a blood path. Some they were able to save but there were those who weren't, and the state of Arizona would never be the same. Sean had no idea of what Norman had planned this go-around, but whatever it was, he knew it wasn't going to be good. Death was surely inevitable if he was involved.

Sean thought taking out the second-in-command had crippled the organization, but now it seemed like they were back with even more treacherous things in mind.

"Your buddy there, Troy, has something implanted in him that may have the answers so if I were you, I would make sure he sought medical attention." With that, Norman hung up.

Troy's hand flew to his right shoulder. He took the shirt off.

Jason examined it. "There's an insertion."

Troy said, "Dial 972-555-9492 for me."

Fifteen minutes later, Sean was driving Troy to one of the local hospitals. Troy's contact would be the one to remove the insertion in a secure and safe room.

Sean said, "Man, you need to call Savannah. She's worried sick about you."

"What if what's in my arm is deadly? I don't know if I can take seeing a worried look on her face. It may be best for her to think that I was still held hostage."

"Okay, I know that thing in your arm must be messing with your brain, because, man, that's just ludicrous."

"Man, I love that woman more than anything in this world. I've already caused her enough pain. It may be best that she finds her someone else," Troy said while looking out the window.

"Delusions must be another sign of what's planted in your arm. Good thing we just pulled up in front of the hospital."

Sean parked the car and he and Troy went to the basement floor of the hospital as instructed. Waiting for them was a tall, lanky dude in a white lab coat. Troy made the introductions.

"Sean, this is Doctor Menchan. I met him while working the Manking assignment."

Dr. Menchan responded, "I love seeing you but not under these circumstances."

"Ditto," the doctor gave Sean a mask to put on. "Just in case," he said.

The doctor and his assistant put on masks. Troy lay on the operating table on his side.

While Troy was distracted, Sean called Montana. "Good news. Troy's alive."

The excitement coming from Montana made Sean glad he called. He continued, "We're at the hospital now getting him checked out. Tell Savannah. I didn't want her to worry another minute."

"What hospital?" Montana asked.

"That I can't tell you. I will call you when he gets out of surgery."

"Surgery? What kind of surgery?" Montana asked.

"I'll tell you everything later. I got to go. Just let her know. Please." Sean ended the call before he blurted out their location. When it came to Montana, he was weak and he wasn't afraid to admit it.

Sean waited outside of the surgery room while the doctor removed the tracking device.

~ 15 ~

The safe house was in a secluded neighborhood. To gain access a person had to stop at the guard shack. The house looked like any other house except it had bulletproof windows and each room had weapons just in case whoever was in the safehouse got ambushed. There was also twenty-four hour security.

Montana watched Savannah toss and turn in the strange bed. She didn't want to disturb her but maybe she would rest better if she knew Troy was safe. "Vanna, wake up." Montana gently shook her.

Savannah shot straight up in the bed. Fear filled her eyes. "What! What!"

"Calm down, sis. I have good news."

"I could use some good news. I kept having this nightmare of Troy."

Montana didn't allow her to continue. "Troy's been located. He's in surgery right now but as soon as Sean knows something he is going to call me back."

Savannah's legs fell to the side of the bed. She looked for her shoes. "I can't just sit here. I got to get to him."

"I don't know what hospital so we need to chill until Sean calls me back."

Savannah screamed, "Get Sean on the phone pronto!"

Montana obeyed her older sister and dialed Sean's number, but was unsuccessful in reaching him. Her back-to-back calls were all going straight to voice mail. Something told her that Sean didn't want to be reached, or he was sending all of her calls to voice mail manually.

Montana's role now was to calm her sister down. "Look, Vanna. At least we know he's safe and sound. Lie back down. He's going to need you and you're not going to be any good if you don't get some rest."

Montana needed to take her own advice. It hadn't even been a full twenty-four hours since learning of Savannah and Troy's abduction but her body felt like she had been up for a week.

Montana said, "Let's make a deal. If you lie down, I'll lie down. My phone is right here. Sean promised to call me with an update."

Reluctantly, Savannah got back in the bed.

Montana leaned her head back on the pillow. She closed her eyes and thanked God again for

Savannah being there and also for Troy's safe return. She didn't know when she dozed off but when she woke up, sunlight beamed through the curtains. She turned over but Savannah was no longer lying next to her. Montana had to ask herself if the last twenty-four hours had been a bad dream.

She looked up when the bedroom door opened and Savannah walked in, using a towel to dry her dripping wet hair. "I couldn't sleep anymore so I got up and took me a long shower and washed my hair."

"Is Asia still asleep?" Montana asked.

"No. She's cooking us breakfast."

Montana felt guilty. She was usually the first one up. It had been that way since they were little. She guessed she was more exhausted than she knew. She picked up her phone from the nightstand. There were a couple of missed calls but none from Sean. Several of her employees were wondering if she was coming into the office today.

She called her secretary and told her she would be taking a few days off and decided to follow suit on what Savannah did by taking a bath. She could hear Asia and Savannah talking after she changed into the clothes that were at the safe house. Tonight, she planned on staying at her own house.

She dialed Sean's number. She needed an update. She was tired of waiting. She didn't get a response. The front door flew open. There stood Sean and Troy. She was so happy to see Troy. He had a few bruises and looked a little pale. She ran up to him and hugged her future brother-in-law.

"Troy, I'm so glad to see you."

Savannah must have heard them. She almost knocked Montana over to get to Troy. Montana moved out of the way and watched the happy reunion. Savannah couldn't take her hands off Troy's face. Troy couldn't take his hands off her face.

"Thanks for making my sister happy," Montana said to Sean.

Sean grabbed Montana's hand and led her into another room. "I'm sorry about not calling you back. Troy had to have emergency surgery."

"Troy looks fine now. What kind of surgery did he have?" Montana asked.

"A chip was placed in him. The doctor ran some tests to make sure there weren't any chemicals in his system. I'm glad to report there weren't any. I heard that Asia is good with computers so we're going to need her to help us decode some things that are on the chip."

"She's a computer guru. That's probably why her and Mike get along. They are both geeks."

"She's a pretty geek."

"Oh, so you've been checking out my sister?" Montana tilted her head to the side and raised her right eye.

"Jealous are we?" Sean asked.

"Never that," Montana said as she crossed her arms.

"I love to see you pout. Come here." Sean didn't wait for her permission. He pulled her in his arms and for a third time kissed her like there was no tomorrow.

Montana's hand fell down to her side. She reached her arms around his neck and pulled him closer. Their tongues danced in and out of each other's mouths. The room spun as Montana got lost in Sean's kiss. If she hadn't known better, she could have sworn she heard Sean moan, or were the moans coming from her?

Sean broke their kiss. "Montana, when I get around you I lose all self-control."

"I'm the one who's usually in control. I wasn't expecting all of this. We barely know anything about each other," Montana said.

"Then I say after all of this is over, we should," Sean responded.

"It's a date." Montana smiled. "Now let's go find Asia so we can see what's on the disk."

Montana left the room knowing that Sean was watching her. She couldn't help but smile.

~ 16 ~

"Did you cook enough for two hungry fellows?" Sean asked as Asia slipped the chip into the device on the computer.

"I cooked enough to feed an army. You'll have to warm it up though," she responded.

"I'm going to do that. I'll be right back." Sean left Asia alone and went to the kitchen. He didn't realize how hungry he was until now. He piled his plate full of food and warmed it up in the microwave.

Asia had a perplexed look on her face. He tried to stay out of her way and keep conversation to a minimum because he didn't like to be bothered whenever he was troubleshooting something.

He ate his food, hoping Asia would be able to figure out what was on the disk.

"Sean, I think I got it," she said.

He placed the plate on the table in front of him and went to stand behind her.

She pointed at the screen. "This is a formula or something." Asia used the mouse and scrolled down on the screen. "Oh my God." Her hand flew to her mouth.

"Let me get here," Sean said as he read over her shoulder.

He and Asia switched positions. Sean pulled out his cell phone. "The battery's dead. Can I borrow your phone?" he asked.

Asia pulled her phone from her pocket and handed it to him. He dialed Mike's number. "Mike, we got a serious problem. Norman is planning on using biological warfare chemicals. Right now what I don't know is if it's going to be airborne, or how he plans on using it."

Mike responded, "Let me get some experts rounded up. Meet me at the office ASAP."

Sean said, "In the meantime, I'm going to contact Homeland Security. They need to be aware of what we might be up against."

Asia said, "What can I do?"

"Make a copy of this for me and put it on one of these flash drives. We're going to keep the original."

"How many copies?"

Sean got out of the chair so Asia could do what he asked. "For now, make three."

Sean went back into the room where Savannah, Troy, and Montana were. "I got word that your places are safe. Troy, I think it's best that you stay either with me or here at this safe house."

Montana said, "They can stay with me. There's plenty of room."

Troy looked at Savannah. "Works for me," Savannah said.

"Now that's settled, as soon as Asia finishes, I'm going to drop you all off and head to the office."

Asia entered the room and handed Sean the flash drives. She then placed the small chip in his other hand. "Did you tell them?" she asked Sean.

Sean hadn't, and had planned on doing so when they were in the car. "Not yet, but we can discuss it on the way to Montana's. I need to hurry up and get to the office."

After everyone was comfortably in the SUV, Sean got everyone up to speed.

Troy said, "It's going to be the water supply. Now everything makes sense." Troy recalled hearing a conversation when his captors thought he was unconscious after one of their beatings. "I heard Norman mention something about 'if we can get them to drink it, it'll work faster.' It has to be what they were speaking of."

Sean and Troy double-checked to make sure Montana's place was secure before allowing them inside. Sean said, "One of our men will be watching the house at all times. I don't want any of you to worry."

Troy said, "Sean, I'm going with you."

Savannah tried to plead with Troy to stay, but he wasn't having it. "I will be back. If anything happens, I'll call you."

Savannah pouted. Sean left them to work things out on their own. He said his good-byes to Asia and Montana. Montana looked like she wanted to say something else, but she didn't.

Troy met him at the car. Troy said, "Mike wants us to meet him at the Federal Building on Midway. Homeland Security has a lot of questions for us."

Sean eased the SUV into busy Dallas traffic on Lyndon B. Johnson Freeway. "I'm hoping Norman calls me back. Man, this can cause an epidemic beyond anything we've ever seen," he admitted.

When they arrived, Sean removed his weapon and placed it in his glove compartment. They went through the normal security and were led to the fifth floor of the Federal Building. When he and Troy entered the room through a gray steel door, already seated inside were three men in dark blue suits, and a woman, with her hair in a bun, wearing a brown suit.

"Have a seat, gentlemen," one of the men said.

Sean looked at Troy right before they both took seats.

The man who had told them to take a seat introduced himself. "I'm Agent Sleeves and we understand you have some information that we need."

Troy took the lead while Sean tried to assess the people in the room. Although they were supposed to have the same goals to catch the bad guys, Sean learned a long time ago that everyone wasn't trustworthy. Some would have their own personal agendas and didn't care who they hurt to achieve them, Troy briefly told them what had transpired in the last twenty-four hours.

Agent Sleeves said, "We should have been informed."

"Agent Sleeves, my team was more than capable of handling the situation," Troy said.

Sean took that moment to interject. "Look, we can go back and forth on this, or we can work together and share information so we can avoid a catastrophic situation."

Sean retrieved one of the flash drives and placed it in front of Agent Sleeves. "This is what they plan to use. Like Mike informed you, they plan on putting this in the water supply. When? We don't know. That's why we're contacting you."

Agent Sleeves handed it to one of the other men in the room. He placed the flash drive in the laptop that was sitting in front of him. He said, "I just sent the info to Davis. He'll be able to tell us exactly what it is."

"Driskoll is behind this. I know for a fact because Norman has been in contact with me. Troy here has confirmed it as well."

"Driskoll was disbanded," Agent Sleeves stated in a matter-of-fact voice.

"Disbanded and now back with even more sinister things in mind," Sean added.

Troy looked down at his new phone. He used one hand to scroll through the numbers in his history on the phone. "Agent Sleeves, we need your people to brief the mayor of Dallas, and the surrounding area representatives, of a possible danger."

"If we do that, we'll have mass panic. Until we know more, I think it's best that we keep this information under wraps."

Sean disagreed. "We're not sure if Driskoll hasn't already set things in motion." Sean pulled out his phone. "Norman wants me to give him ten million dollars, but that's not going to stop him from doing what he plans."

"Driskoll is not a threat. My men will see to that," Agent Sleeves boasted.

"Driskoll is not just one person but a team of people who will do whatever Norman tells them. Right now he's angry and he's set to make DFW an example of what his ultimate goal is, and that's to bring the people of our great country to their knees. As a soldier, I cannot and I will not let that happen. So I'm asking—no, I'm begging— you to do as Troy has asked so we can all work together and save the citizens of this great city." Something Sean said must have softened Agent Sleeves' stance. He saw him lean over to the man seated to his right side and whisper. The guy got up and left the room.

"He'll take care of that. In the meantime, we need for you two to tell us as much as you can."

Sean leaned over the desk and shared as much as he cared to share with the Feds.

~ 17 ~

Montana eased her body down in the hot
bubbling water. She exhaled as she felt the
tension leave her body as she lowered herself
into the tub.

All was well in her world at this moment in
time. Savannah was safe. Nothing else mattered. She leaned back in the tub and closed her
eyes. Visions of Sean filled her thoughts. She
smiled as she reminisced about their kisses.
Whenever they kissed, the world seemed to get
small and they were the only two who mattered.

Her hand eased its way underneath the bub-
bles. Her body temperature rose as she thought
about Sean touching her in her most intimate
spots. Her hand eased in between her legs. She
imagined Sean planting kisses. She moaned
as the heat built up in her body. She used her
fingers to pleasure herself as she called Sean's
name out loud several times while reaching
a climax.

A knock on the door broke the trance she was under. Asia yelled from the other side, "Montana, are you okay in there? You've been in there an awfully long time."

Montana chuckled. Asia would mess up a wet dream. "I'm fine. I'll be out shortly," she yelled loud enough for Asia to hear her.

Montana washed off and dressed in something comfortable. Both of her sisters were sitting in the living room. Savannah lay on the couch, staring at the ceiling. Asia sat on the loveseat with a laptop in her lap.

"What's up?" Montana said, as she plopped down right beside Asia.

"I'm trying to look up more information on those people who took Vanna. And, sis, there's a lot of bad stuff here."

"Like what? Tell me something I don't already know," Montana said as she leaned over so she could also see the computer screen.

"Driskoll is some rogue organization who blames the government for everything. They went on a killing spree in Arizona a few years ago. Remember the time when a lot of the mayors of towns in that state were targeted? Well, Driskoll is the organization behind it."

"Wow. That's why I'm thanking God that Vanna and Troy made it out safely."

"Driskoll is the name of the founder who died right before they did the Arizona massacre. Sean was one of the ones instrumental in capturing who was said to be the mastermind behind the plan. Up until yesterday, Driskoll had been quiet," Asia said.

"I wonder why they chose to do something now," Montana commented.

Savannah sat up. "There's something I need to tell you."

Montana and Asia both looked in Savannah's direction. Savannah continued, "Although I wasn't physically tortured, I was mentally. They sat me in a chair and the moment I sat down on it, a bomb was activated."

Montana felt a panic attack coming on, but took a few deep breaths to calm down. "Are you serious?"

Savannah said, "Very much so. If Sean didn't know how to deactivate it, I wouldn't be sitting here with you now. It's possible he and I would have blown up when that building exploded."

Montana said, "Thank you, God," several times.

"That Norman guy is pure evil. His eyes were coal black and empty. I swear it looked like he didn't have a soul behind those eyes." Savannah's body shivered as she spoke about him.

"We can't just sit back and let him get away with this," Montana said.

Asia stated, "Let's let Troy, Sean, and Mike handle this. They are the experts."

Montana disagreed. "I know but, sis, there has to be something we can do."

Savannah said, "There is. I think I know where he's going."

"We need to call Sean and Troy and let them know, Vanna."

Asia pulled out her phone. "Call them."

Montana dialed Sean's number but kept getting his voice mail. "What's Troy's number?"

"I don't have his new number," she responded.

"Dial 972-555-2030," Asia said.

"Hello, you've reached the right number but at the wrong time. Please leave a message," Mike's voice mail recording said.

Montana handed Asia back her phone. "Okay, nobody's answering their phone. Let's get dressed and head to their office."

"I guess we're riding with you since I have no car," Asia said.

Savannah asked, "Where's your car?"

Asia looked at Montana. "Should I tell her, or do you want to tell her?"

Montana gestured that the floor was hers. She left the room to find her shoes as Asia informed

Savannah of Asia's car exploding. When she
made it back downstairs they were waiting for
her at the front door.

"Maybe we should check your car for a bomb
too," Savannah said with a serious face.

Montana's heart went out to her sister. Her
ordeal had to have been traumatizing. "Everything's okay. Remember, the guys had everything
checked out."

They slipped into the car. She waved at one
of Troy's men as she backed out of the driveway.
Thirty minutes later she was at the gate of Troy
and Sean's office. The guard recognized them,
but asked, "Are they expecting you?"

"No, but . . ." Montana responded.

Asia leaned over and said, "Call Mike and tell
him we're here."

The guard talked into his phone but in a
low voice. He released the button to the gate.
"Someone will escort you inside."

Montana drove through the gate and parked
in the nearest empty parking spot. Mike met
them at the door.

"I thought I told y'all to stay off your phone,"
Sean said, looking directly at Montana.

Montana twisted her chair around. "Last
time I checked, I was grown woman and I can
do whatever I please."

"You are grown, aren't you?" Sean said as he
tilted his lip.

Troy cleared his throat. "Sean, maybe you could"

~ 18 ~

Sean and Troy were at the Federal Building
for at least five hours sharing information with
the agents and trying to devise a plan that they
both were satisfied with. When they were getting
back in Sean's car, that's when he realized he
had some missed calls. Several of them were
from Montana. He dialed her number right
away.

He was happy to know they were okay but
wasn't too happy to find out they were at the
office. He got off the phone with Montana and
said. "Those three are going to be a problem,"
Sean said to Troy.

"Stubborn and the Blake sisters go hand in
hand."

"I see that," Sean said as he drove to the office.

When they arrived, Sean eased into the closest
parking spot he could find.

The ladies were so wrapped up in what was
on the computer screen that none realized they
were no longer alone.

"I thought I told y'all to stay at your place," Sean said, looking directly at Montana.

Montana swiveled her chair around. "Last time I checked, I was a grown woman and could do whatever I please."

"You are definitely all woman," Sean said as he licked his lips.

Troy cleared his throat. "Savannah, you should be home resting. You've had a grueling twenty-four hours."

"And so have you. More so than me and you haven't gotten any sleep yet," Savannah noted.

"I will in due time," he responded.

Asia interrupted, "Hey, I know all of you love-birds are a little testy right now but we got some important things going on."

Asia handed Sean a printout. Sean didn't want to know how Asia was able to tap in to what was supposed to be confidential information. She was Major's daughter so that was all the answer he needed.

The information on the print out wasn't a surprise. He and Troy had just been debriefed on it by the Feds. Details of some of Driskoll's past crimes as well as information the Feds received from an informant of some future plots Driskoll had planned to execute were listed. The list only confirmed what Sean already knew. Driskoll was a psychopath that needed to be off the streets.

Sean's phone rang. He noticed the same strange "999" number so he knew it had to be Norman. He hit the speaker button.

"I see you've been talking to the Feds," Norman was no longer using the computer generated voice, as he spoke on the other end of the phone.

"Norman, you left me no choice. We got the chip you implanted in Troy's arm."

"You were supposed to find that after I delivered Troy's dead body to your doorstep." Norman sounded disappointed.

"This has to end."

"I promise you if you give me the money and meet some of my other demands that nothing will happen. I will have my men destroy the vials and we both can go on living our happy lives."

"I have the ten million dollars but there's one problem," Sean said.

"And what's that?" Norman asked.

"I don't know if I can trust you. How do I know you won't pull the okey-doke on me?"

"You don't. But I'm telling you, I may be many things, Sean, but a liar is not one of them."

Sean eased in the chair so he could get more comfortable. "Everyone lies, Norm."

"It's Norman. Have some manners." Norman sounded agitated.

"Norm, tell me, how can I guarantee you won't go ahead with your plans?"

"You're not going to ask me what my other demands are, Sean? Don't you want to know?"

"At this point, does it really matter?"

"Do you not care about people?"

"Look. Norm. I'm tired of playing this game with you. It's getting old. Either you're going to give me something I can work with, or you can forget everything."

Norman laughed out loud. Then they all heard a loud boom as if he slammed his hand against something. "You've forgotten who is in control. The same way I got to your friend is the same way I can get to you. Do you think you can really stop me from doing what I want to do? No. I have people in many places. How do you think I found out about you, Sean? Answer that."

Sean wanted to know how he knew about the bond he and Troy shared. Did they have a mole among them? Sean didn't want to doubt anyone on their team, but in this line of business, sometimes money overrode loyalty.

Sean said in a calm voice, "Norman, you're right. You have all of the control right now. All I want to do is make sure you get what you want and I get what I want. And what I want is for the citizens of this city to be safe."

"They will be, if you abide by my wishes."

Sean stated, "I know you want the ten million dollars. What are your other demands?"

Mike mouthed the words, "Got him."

Norman said, "I want you."

Sean remained quiet. Norman kept talking. "I want you and that will save the people. Are you prepared to be a sacrifice for millions, Sean?"

Troy shook his head no, but Sean ignored him. "When do you want this transaction to take place?"

"Tomorrow. I will call you back with the time and location."

"Before that happens, I need some assurance that we get all of the vials you have and that you will call off your whole operation of poisoning the water system."

"Sean, you have my word. I will leave the vials in a black suitcase at the designated location for one of your comrades to get. But, Sean, if I think there's any funny business going on, not only will I kill you, but we will move forward with our plans and then your death would be in vain. And we don't want that to be the case, now do we?"

Sean knew that he was embarking on something dangerous. He had to do whatever he could to save lives. He made that vow when he became a member of the military, special forces, and when he decided to join Troy in their security operations firm. "I will do whatever I need to do to save the people."

"Glad to hear that, Sean. I will call you back at zero nine hundred tomorrow for further instructions. Remember, no funny business or not only are you dead, but many others will die along with you."

Norman hung up the phone without waiting for Sean to respond.

Sean looked up at the scared look in Montana's eyes. That was the first time in his career that he felt bad about putting his life on the line.

~ 19 ~

Montana felt a panic attack coming on. She was normally calm but with Savannah being abducted and now Sean putting his life on the line, she just couldn't take it. She felt herself hyperventilating.

Sean jumped up out of his chair and ran to her side. Asia rushed out of the room and quickly returned with a cup of water. Montana put her head between her legs and took in a few deep breaths as she was taught to do by their dad. She hadn't experienced panic attacks since she was a little girl. Now they were back.

Once she was able to get some form of control, she sat up in her seat and saw several pair of worried eyes staring back at her. She took a sip of the water Asia gave her. "I'm sorry I scared y'all. I'm okay."

Sean placed his arm around her shoulders. "See, that's why you should have stayed at home. This is a dangerous thing. I should have taken the call in private."

"You don't have to risk your life. We can come up with another way. We have to. I'm just getting to know you. I can't lose you," Montana blurted out.

Sean looked at everyone else in the room. "Can you give us a few minutes alone?"

Savannah hugged Montana before leaving. So did Asia. Once everyone was out of the room, Sean took Montana in his arms. "I have a confession to make. I love you, Montana."

"No, you don't, Sean. You don't know me enough to say that."

"I fell in love with you the first time I saw you," Sean confessed.

"But—" Montana said.

"There's no buts. I love you. I'm in love with you and that's why I got to do what I got to do. I wouldn't be able to look in your eyes if I didn't do all I could to save the people."

"But you don't have to do this. Who is to say he won't still poison the water supply? Sean, please don't do this."

Sean's eyes got watery. "Baby, please don't cry." Sean used one of his hands and wiped the tears from Montana's eyes.

Montana pulled away. "This is so unlike me. Who am I kidding? This is what you do. You love risking your life."

"I wish there was another way around it. If there was, I wouldn't go this route."

"There has to be another way," Montana responded.

Sean said, "Let me take care of some things here and tonight it will be just you and me. At your place, though, because I'm not sure if going to my place is entirely safe."

Montana had to be satisfied with that for now.

Montana, when upset, liked to cook and clean. After returning home, to her sisters' dismay, she went on a cleaning frenzy. With plastic gloves on and disinfectant in her hands, Montana cleaned all of the bathrooms. Once she was through with the bathrooms, she vacuumed the rooms with carpet. She seemed to go over the same spot over and over with the dust rag as she tried to de-stress. She had to think of something to keep her mind off the possibility of losing Sean to the maniac who had kidnapped Savannah.

Montana decided to cook a roast and potatoes so she put those in the stove before going back to the dusting.

Savannah entered the dining room, where Montana was dusting, and said, "Sean will be here shortly. Why don't you go shower and put on something sexy for him? We promise to stay out of your way. In fact, we're going to Asia's so you can have the place to yourself."

Montana felt bad. Here she was forgetting about Savannah's ordeal and being really selfish with her own life. "Y'all don't have to. This house is big enough for all of us."

"I think it's best. We'll be gone by the time you get out of the bathroom. I'll make sure things are locked and secure."

An hour later, Montana walked down the stairs in a simple yet sexy black fitted dress and high heels. She glanced at herself in the side mirror. She laughed when she saw how her sisters had the dining room fixed up for a romantic dinner for two.

"When did they have time to do this?"

Montana had cooked and the food was still warming. She hadn't heard from Sean so she wasn't exactly sure of what time to expect him. Apparently Savannah and Asia did, because as she was admiring the nice place settings, the doorbell rang.

Out of habit, she looked through the peephole before acknowledging the person on the other side. Sean's beautiful face was on the other side. Montana ran her hand down her dress and opened the door.

Sean handed her a bouquet of roses. "Troy told me I better clean up a little, so how do you like?" he said as he entered and kissed her on the cheek.

"You clean up well," Montana responded as she placed the flowers on the table in the foyer.

"You're beautiful. Simply beautiful," Sean said as she led him to the dining room.

"Dinner is ready so we might as well eat up," Montana said. She needed to do something to distract her from the heat that filled her body.

They both played a little cat and mouse game over dinner. Sean shared some stories from his college days with Troy. Montana said, "I'm surprised you don't remember my sister. She and Troy were a hot item from what I understand."

"Troy kept Savannah pretty much to himself. I met her but didn't spend too much time around her. In fact, your sister sort of kidnapped my friend. I resented her a little at first, truth be told."

"Well, that'll be our little secret." Montana winked her eye before taking a bite of the apple pie she cooked for dessert.

"As good as your apple pie is, I can think of another dessert I want," Sean stated.

Montana licked her lips. "Oh, really?"

Sean eased the chair back. He held his hand out. Montana reached for his hand and got up. It was as if Sean had her under some type of spell. He wrapped one arm around her waist and used the other hand and tilted Montana's head. He bent down and whispered in her ear, "Tonight, I want to make you mine."

Montana didn't protest. "Follow me," she said.

Sean's arm dropped to the side. Montana held on to one hand as she led him up the stairs to her bedroom.

Before they got into the room good they were devouring each other's mouths as their tongues did a dance of their own darting in and out of each one of their mouths. Moans were heard coming from both of them.

Montana pulled the dress over her head and revealed her curvaceous body. Desire filled Sean's eyes as he stood and admired her beauty. She then removed the clip from her hair and her beautiful spiral curls fell to her shoulders

She used her index finger and motioned for him to come closer. He did as he was told. When he reached her, Montana stared Sean in the eyes as she used her hands to unbuckle his belt. She undid the button.

She sat on the bed as Sean pulled off his slacks. He leaned down and Montana fell back on the bed. Their lips reconnected. Sean planted kisses on her neck, and when he reached her chest, he gently caressed each one of her breasts with his fingers and lips. Montana's body trembled with desire.

20

Sean couldn't get enough of kissing Montana in some of her most intimate places. The moans coming from her only excited him more. He was feening to taste her sweet nectar. His lips found the nectar he'd been craving. Montana's legs gripped around Sean's neck as he drove her to ecstasy.

"Seannnnn," she moaned as he brought her to a climax.

Not able to withstand being inside her much longer, Sean eased up from in between her legs. He reached into his pants pocket and pulled out a condom from his wallet. He watched the desire seep from Montana's eyes as he slid the condom on. He used his hand and gently opened up her legs. He "ahhed" the moment he entered her.

Their bodies rocked back and forth as he closed his eyes and got lost in her sweetness. "I love you," he moaned as Montana wrapped her legs around him.

"I love you too," Montana responded in between moans.

That was all he needed to hear. The sound of her confessed love pushed him over the edge and he let out a howl as he climaxed.

He held on to Montana real tight. He never wanted to let her go. Montana laid her head on his bare chest as he ran his fingers through her disheveled hair.

"You're the best thing that's ever happened to me," Sean said.

Montana looked up into his eyes. "That's sweet of you to say."

"I'm only telling you the truth. Sweetheart, I know we've only really gotten to know each other in a record two days, but you're everything I've always wanted." Sean kissed Montana on her forehead.

"Savannah is the one who reads those mushy romance novels so I don't normally believe in love at first sight, but with you, you've made it possible for me to love again. That's why I don't want to see you endanger your life with that Norman guy." After realizing Dion, her ex-boyfriend, was insane, Montana had vowed off men.

"Montana, shh. Tonight is our night." Sean's body had rejuvenated itself.

This time, Montana took the lead and control. She raised herself on top of his body and planted kisses all over his chest. "Love me like you've never loved before," Montana said in a seductive voice. She rode him bareback. Sean didn't even think about not having a condom when he released his seeds inside of Montana. Montana collapsed on top of his chest. They slept in that position until the next morning.

Sean didn't want to wake Montana up, but a quick glance at the clock showed that it was almost eight o'clock in the morning. He wanted to be showered and dressed when he got the call from Norman. He gently slid Montana's body off him and onto the bed. She yawned, but didn't wake up fully.

He was lathering up the soap on his body when the shower curtain opened. Montana stepped in. She took the washcloth away from him and washed his body. This selfless act touched Sean's heart. He returned the favor and washed her all over. When his hand reached in between her legs, he couldn't resist pleasuring her.

Before long, he had Montana penned up against the shower wall and entered her in a quick jolt. They made love again as if their entire lives depended on it as the water from the shower ran down their bodies.

They dried off in silence and got dressed. Montana wore a pair of slacks and nice satin blouse. While she was dressing, he retrieved a duffle bag from his car and came back in and changed into a pair of jeans and a button-down shirt.

Montana met him at the bottom of the stairs. "While we're waiting on the call, I think I'll cook you a hearty breakfast."

It didn't take Montana long to whip up a breakfast fit for a king. While they were eating, her doorbell rang.

"I'll be right back," she said.

Just in case it was an uninvited guest, Sean placed his hand on his waistband where his weapon was holstered. He was prepared to pull it out just in case.

He heard familiar voices so he eased up and removed his hand from his waist. The whole gang was now there: her sisters, Mike, and Troy, and Jason had also followed them in.

"Any more grub, sis?" Troy asked.

"Somehow, I knew I would need more, so eat up," Montana said, as she reentered the dining room with trays of food.

They sat around the table and served themselves.

Sean grabbed Montana's hand and pulled her to the side. "I love you."

"I love you too." Montana asked, "Do you think they can tell that we, well, you know."

"It's written all over your face."

Montana's hand flew to her face. "Are you serious?"

Sean couldn't help but laugh as he pulled her closer to him. "I'm kidding. We're grown, they're grown, I'm sure they know we probably did what grown folks do."

"But still. I'm a private person. I don't like everybody up in my business," Montana said.

"You'll live," Sean responded.

"But . . . I normally don't jump head first into a relationship. I usually know the guy for some time." Montana frowned.

"Technically, we met three years ago." Sean attempted to rationalize with Montana. The last thing he wanted was for her to feel guilty about him and the lovemaking they shared earlier and the night before. The love he had for her was deep and the sex only intensified the level of his feelings.

He felt the phone in his pants vibrate before it started ringing out loud. Montana eased out of his arms. He took the phone out of his pocket. It was Norman.

"Everybody, this is Norman," Sean said as he and Montana went back into the dining room.

Montana handed him a notepad as he clicked the on button and speaker button on his phone.

"It's a beautiful day in the neighborhood," Norman sang from the other end of the phone. "Sean, are you there?"

"I'm right here," Sean said in a nonchalant voice.

"Do you have my money ready?" Norman asked.

"Yes."

"Good. I want you to meet my man in the West End at eleven hundred. Come alone because I have eyes everywhere. He'll give you your next set of instructions then."

"Before I do that, where will the vials be?"

"My man will give you that information when you meet him there. I suggest you say your good-byes. Sean, I'm proud of you. You're saving plenty of lives." Norman laughed and hung up the phone.

Troy said, "Man, I have a bad feeling about this."

Sean tried not to show fear. "He'll have his men watching me, but we'll get our men in place."

Mike was already on his phone. "That's less than two hours but we'll be ready."

Sean said, "Fellows, I'll meet you outside. Just want to talk to Montana by myself."

Sean's heart tore in pieces when he saw the tears stream down Montana's beautiful oval face.

21

Montana felt like she was being punished for a past sin. She had waited all of her life to find a love like Sean's. Now that she was open to dating again, fate would have it that he would be taken away from her.

Sean wiped her face. "Baby, please don't cry."

Montana rubbed his face. "I'll be all right. You do what you must and know that no matter what happens I love you."

"I love you too," Sean said as he pulled her into his arms.

Their hug was interrupted by Jason's voice. "Sean, it's time."

Sean pulled away. "I got to go. I'll call you from the car, okay?"

Montana kissed Sean for what could be the last time. She followed him to the front door. Her sisters stood by her side as she waved good-bye as the two cars that were in the driveway eased away.

As soon as she closed the door, Savannah said, "So what do we do next?"

Montana looked perplexed. "Sitting and waiting is not an option. "

They went to the living room. Montana took a seat on the couch and crossed her legs.

Asia, holding her iPad, said, "Well, I have a few apps here that will help us see what's going on in the West End."

Savannah added, "However, I think we can move this party to one of the restaurants."

Asia batted her eyes. "It's a nice day to sit out on the patio, don't you think?"

"Savannah, you can't go out looking like that. He said his people will be there, so of course they know how you look."

Savannah got up and reached for Montana's hand. "Well, that means you need to get busy, because we don't have much time."

Montana transformed Savannah's long hair into a crop, where she and Asia almost looked identical. With shades on and the darker makeup, no one would be able to tell Savannah. Montana decided to give herself a quick makeover too just in case they had been watching Sean and knew how she looked. Montana added several tracks into her hair increasing its fullness. She used makeup to lighten up her complexion.

Asia retrieved a black duffle bag filled with surveillance devices provided by Mike during some of their previous tactical training. "Let's go," Asia said as she gripped the handles of the bag.

Savannah said, "We can go in my car. It has speed just in case we need it."

Montana agreed. "Well, let's go."

Savannah lucked out and found a parking place not far from the restaurant they were going to use for their own personal stakeout. They were all dressed like businesswomen who were there for lunch.

Asia requested a seat out on the patio. Her sunglasses were specially made with cameras. With the small control she had at her fingertips, she zoomed in and out as she needed to.

Although none of the ladies were hungry they ordered to keep up their pretense. They each played over their food as they played the waiting game.

Savannah said, "I think they are here. Look at six o'clock."

Without being obvious, Montana glanced in the direction. Montana's heart skipped a beat. "Oh, my God. There he is."

Neither Asia nor Savannah had to ask who because they knew it was Sean.

Asia had scanned the area and taken snapshots of faces of different people, and ran them through a security program. Unfortunately, although some did come back with some criminal backgrounds, none were part of the fascist organization Norman was a part of until Montana heard Asia say, "Bingo."

"What?" Montana asked, although never taking her eyes off Sean. She hoped he didn't look in her direction. He kept walking. He paused for a moment and turned, and Montana held her menu up so he couldn't see her.

"That was close," Montana whispered.

Sean kept walking to his destination.

"We have our guy," Asia said.

Sean sat down at a reserved seat nearby. No one was at the table. His back was toward them. Montana was relieved. Her cell phone vibrated. It was a text message from Sean.

It read: I luv U.

She sent him a quick text message back: I luv U more.

He responded with a smiley face.

Montana slipped her phone back in her pocket. "At first I thought he was on to us," she confessed to her sisters.

The guy who Asia pinpointed as being with Norman got up from his seat. He held a newspaper close to his body. He greeted Sean.

Asia used the device located on the tip of the ear of her glasses to amplify the sound so she could listen in. She repeated what she heard to Montana and Savannah. "He wants Sean to go to some place in Fort Worth. I'm Googling it now."

"When?" Montana asked.

"He's giving him one hour to get there. The newspaper he's handing him has instructions on where the poisonous vials will be."

"Can you see that?"

"No. The way Sean is sitting, it's blocking my view," Asia responded.

"I think we need to get going, ladies," Savannah said.

The waiter hadn't returned with their food yet but Montana reached in her purse and left two twenty dollar bills. He could trash it, or give the food to someone else.

"Hey, your meals," she heard the waiter yell as they rushed away.

She hoped that Sean hadn't noticed their quick departure.

Once they were securely in Savannah's car and on the road, Montana's phone rang. Sean's number showed in the display. "I want you to know I knew that was you in that short hair disguise."

Montana had been outed. "We didn't get in the way. I just had to see you one more time," she assured him.

"Anything could have happened. Montana, go home. I got this."

"But—"

"But nothing. I don't want to be worried about you. Promise me."

Montana crossed her fingers. "Scout's honor," she responded.

"I will call you as soon as I can. Troy needs my line open. Love you."

"I love you too," Montana said.

She hated lying to Sean, but there was no way she was going home. With her two sisters by her side, she was going to do whatever she had to do to help protect her man.

~ 22 ~

Sean didn't know what Montana was thinking showing up at the West End. All of their lives could have been in jeopardy. Thankfully, the only thing that happened was the handler passed him the information on his next stop.

Troy's number flashed across Sean's cell phone display. "I got the location and we're headed to that direction now."

"Good. Your girl and her sisters were at the West End."

"Where are they now?" Troy asked.

"Montana promised me they were going to stay out of this."

"For their sake, I hope they do," Troy responded.

Sean and Troy went back and forth on the strategy they would use. "Man, if I don't come out of this alive, I want my ashes spread."

Troy interrupted him. "We're not even having this conversation. We're going to do as planned. Get those vials and you'll be romancing your girl before morning."

Sean eased the negative thoughts out of his mind as he continued on Interstate 20 toward Fort Worth. Once he was alerted that all of the men were in place, Sean felt a little more at ease. He hit the volume on his stereo and T.I.'s song "Motivation" blasted.

Sean eased his car in the empty parking spot behind the warehouse. He checked out his environment. "Guys, where you at? Use a flash to let me know."

He saw a quick flash. He confidently unbuckled his seatbelt and opened his door. The walk from his car to the warehouse doorway seemed like an eternity. He knocked and the door eased open.

A big, burly man patted him down. "The boss is in the back."

The wire and hidden camera were sewn into Sean's clothes and were able to go undetected. His team should have been able to see and hear whatever he saw. He headed to the room where he would come face to face with Norman.

Two of Norman's soldiers were at the door. They moved and allowed him to enter. The warehouse looked more like a chop shop for cars, Sean noticed as he walked through into one huge room. He saw the back of a big white cowboy hat.

The chair swiveled around. Norman was older than Sean had imagined. This was the first time he had ever seen him. All other pictures they had of him were fuzzy. He looked like a younger version of Colonel Sanders, but plumper.

Sean stood in a strong stance. "So we finally meet."

"I see you really do have a heart. I was beginning to wonder for a minute there," Norman said as he stood up, holding his pearl-handled walking cane.

"I'm here. Now what's next?" Sean asked, without blinking.

"Where's the money?"

"It's safe and secure. As soon as we get the vials, you'll get the ten million."

"You know I can have my men take you out right now, but what's the point? Then you wouldn't be able to keep me company."

"Norm . . . I can call you Norm, can't I?" Sean asked.

"It's Norman and you have one more time to disrespect me." The smile on Norman's face disappeared.

"I'm not here to make friends with you. Do what you plan on doing so we can get this over with."

Norman slammed the head of the cane on the table. "You're not the boss of me. I'm the one in control here."

Sean smirked and threw his hands up in the air. "Okay. Understood. This is your show. I'm just here for the ride."

"You got that right. And that's exactly what we're about to do. We're going for a ride. As soon as you give me my money."

"Vials for the money. It's your choice."

Norman pressed a button on the phone on the table. "Leave all of the vials."

"Once my men contact me that they have the vials, I will tell you where the money is."

Norman pulled out a deck of cards from his pocket. "Are you feeling lucky today?"

"I don't believe in luck," Sean said.

"Have a seat. I feel a little lucky."

Sean entertained Norman by agreeing to play poker.

Sean was a good poker player however he gave up some plays to give Norman some confidence.

Norman smiled as he won more and more of Sean's chips. Sean pretended to be disappointed as he studied Norman.

Norman said, "I guess you were too busy working in the field to learn how to play cards, soldier."

Sean said, "I play well enough to give you some competition."

"I'm running circles around you. If we were playing for money, you would be broke."

"Poker is just a game to me."

Norman said, "Poker is a skill. You either have the skills to play or you don't. Obviously, you don't."

Sean's phone rang. "Do you mind if I take this call?"

Norman gestured that it was okay.

Mike said from the other end of the phone. "We got the suitcase with the vials. Send one of your men to my car. The suitcase with the ten million is in the trunk. The button to pop the trunk is located on the driver's side near the steering wheel."

Norman called one of his men on the phone and repeated the instructions. "Bring it directly to me. Pronto," Norman stated. "For your sake, it better all be there."

Sean said, "Like you, I'm a man of my word."

"Well, then we shouldn't have any problems."

"None whatsoever," Sean agreed as he stared Norman straight in the eyes.

The guard entered the room with the two black duffle bags. Norman unzipped them and seemed to be foaming at the mouth at the sight of the twenties that filled the bags. "Tell Chip to come here. I need him to count this. But these bags do not leave this room."

Sean said, "It's been counted twice. It's all there."

Norman and Sean continued their poker game while Chip counted the money. Sean glanced at his watch. He wondered why Norman was stalling by having the man count the money several times. Sean didn't trust Norman not one bit.

Montana didn't like the look on Asia's face. She was on the phone talking to Mike. Savannah had the same worried look. She was on the phone talking to Troy. Montana's heartbeat was so loud, she was surprised no one else could hear it. The suspense of not knowing what was being said was killing her. The only thing either one of her sisters could be heard saying was, "Okay," or, "I see."

They were seated in Savannah's car not far from the warehouse where Sean was being held. Thankfully, Asia was able to get the location of Sean's whereabouts. It had been an hour and there was still no sign of Sean leaving. The waiting game was killing her. She sent Sean a text message, not knowing if he got it. She just wanted him to know that she loved him.

Savannah ended her call with Troy. "Montana, looks like we've been duped. Those vials were nothing but vials of water. Sean's not answering his phone. Troy's trying to plan on what he wants to do next."

Asia was now off her phone call too. "I see the men at the gate. I say we charm our way in. I got my friend's son bringing us pizza. I'll be the pizza delivery girl and while I get the main guard distracted, you two can sneak in."

Savannah frowned. "I'm not sure if we should do that. We don't know who's in that warehouse."

Asia opened up the bag beside her and retrieved several weapons and other paraphernalia from it. "Put this in your ears. One of us needs to be the lookout, so once I finish delivering the pizza that no one really ordered, I'll go back to my car. I'm going to park it a block away so you'll know where it is. In order to keep in communication with each other, put these on. The mic you will clip to your collar."

"But . . ." Savannah hesitated.

"Vanna, if this was Troy, what would you do?" Asia said in an authoritative voice.

Montana didn't wait for Savannah to reply. "I'm tired of waiting. Sean's life could be in danger," Montana responded.

"Exactly, so as your sisters, we're going to help you go get your man," Savannah responded as she clipped on her microphone and put the other chip in her ear.

Montana hesitantly took the devices and put them in similar places. She took two of the guns Asia handed to her. One she strapped around her ankle and the other she held in her hand.

"Here are a few more clips just in case you run out," Asia said.

"This is enough to kill an army," Montana commented.

"Exactly. Believe me, it's better to have too much ammunition than not enough," Savannah said as she got ready to implement their plan.

"There's the pizza," Asia said as a blue car pulled up beside them.

Asia retrieved some money from her purse and handed it to the young college student. They did an even exchange. Besides handing her three boxes of pizza, he gave her a smock with the pizza company's logo on it, and a hat.

"Mama told me to tell you hello," the young eager college boy could be heard saying.

"Tell her I'll call her later," Asia said as she tried to rush him along so they could go on with their plans.

Once they were sure he was gone, Asia changed into the smock and put on the hat. Savannah moved out of the driver's seat and she and Montana both got in the back seat.

"Although your windows are tinted, stay down as we pull up. When I open the back door to get what looks like pizza, that's when you two need to slip out of the car."

Savannah said, "We need a code word to alert us when to make our move."

Asia said, "When I say, 'They are heavy on the pepperoni,' you know it's clear for you to move in."

"Got it," Montana said as she said a silent prayer.

The next few minutes seemed to move in slow motion as Asia parked in front of the warehouse. She opened the door and Savannah and Montana slipped out as discussed. Asia started humming a Whitney Houston song as she walked up the walkway with the pizza.

She rang the doorbell and her head turned around so if they were looking out a peephole, they would see the pizza company logo and her holding the three boxes.

A tall, burly-looking guy opened the door. "We didn't order a pizza."

Asia looked at the ticket. "Somebody from this address ordered a pizza. I'm tired and I'm disgusted so somebody here is going to pay me."

"Did anyone ever tell you, you sort of look like Halle Berry?"

"Sometimes," Asia smiled, as if she were warming up to him.

"But you're prettier than she is."

"Well, thanks. Now are you going to pay for these pizzas or not?" Asia batted her eyes.

"Anything for you, pretty lady." The man pulled out several twenties and handed them to her. "Do you have a man?" he asked.

"No. Why, are you in the market?"

"As a matter of fact, I am. Why don't you let me call you?"

"Why don't you give me your number and I'll think about it?"

"Do you have anything to write with?" he asked.

"No, but my cell phone's in the car. Why don't you walk back with me to my car and I'll program it in my phone."

"Let me take those pizzas from you," he said.

"Please do, and you'll like them because they are heavy on the pepperoni."

He held on to the pizzas as he walked with Asia back to the car.

Savannah and Montana peeked around. While Asia had him occupied, they ran up the walkway and into the warehouse.

Montana whispered, "Now what?"

~ 24 ~

Sean was steaming mad when he heard Troy say in his ear that the vials weren't anything but water. He couldn't play his hand just yet though until he knew Norman's other plans. Norman smiled like a big Cheshire cat. He seemed to get a thrill out of the fact that he got the $10 million. Little did Norman know, however, that the money was marked. Of course, it wasn't going to be obvious, so the moment the money started being spent he, or whoever used the money, would be identified.

Norman sat on the other end of the table and stared at Sean. "Did you actually think you would walk out of here?"

"You got the money. We got the vials, so what's the purpose of holding me?" Sean asked.

Norman laughed. "Sean, did you actually think I would give up the real vials?" Norman leaned back in his chair.

Sean, still trying to mask his anger, said, "I did what you asked, now you need to live up to your end of the bargain."

"I had to make sure you guys didn't renege on your end."

"Where are the vials, Norman?"

"When we move to our next location, your men will get the vials. I didn't want them to try anything funny so I still have them for safe keeping."

Norman pulled out a silver case and opened it. He turned the case around in Sean's direction. "See, these babies here pack a lot of punch. These twelve vials could take out a whole city."

Sean looked at the clear vials filled with what looked like gel.

"Let me show you what it can do," Norman said, as he moved the briefcase away and slammed it shut, right before clicking the lock and placing it right back next to him on the floor.

"Bill, flip the light off and turn the video on," Norman said.

One of the guards did as he was directed. Sean looked at the big-screen monitor and watched someone place the vial in a dish. A lab mouse drank from it and within seconds, it was foaming at the mouth and, just like that, it was dead.

"We then tried it on monkeys," Norman said. He seemed thrilled to watch the screen as it flashed several monkeys drinking from bottles that looked like they were filled with water, but were filled with the contents of the vial.

The same thing happened to the monkeys. They all started foaming at the mouth, but instead of just passing out, they seemed to experience seizures before passing out. A masked man dressed in white checked their pulses and confirmed to the cameras that they were dead.

Norman hit the cordless mouse button. Bill turned the lights back on. "See what could happen if gotten into the water supply?"

Sean didn't want to imagine seeing humans being victims of the madman who sat before him. He hoped that Troy could hear their conversation.

"Let me call my men. If it's more money you want, we'll get it to you."

Norman hit the head of the cane on the table. "I'm the only one who can make demands."

"I'm here. I delivered the money to you. All I want to know is what else you want so we can make this transition as smooth as possible." Sean looked Norman straight in the eyes. He didn't have time to be fearful; instead, he stared fear straight in the face.

"For now, you need to call your team and tell them not to follow us. I'm sure they're outside watching."

"No. I told you I came alone."

"Now, see, our relationship would be better if you wouldn't lie to me, Sean."

Sean saw that he had several missed calls on his phone. He quickly looked at the text message from Montana. He couldn't respond, but seeing her message gave him the will to do whatever he could to survive the predicament he found himself in. He dialed Troy's number.

Troy said, "He tricked us. It was water. Water."

Sean said, "I know. We're sitting here now. He promises to deliver the correct vials once we're secure in another location. He thinks you guys are outside ready to move in on us so once we move, he'll get the correct vials to you."

"That's enough. Now hang up," Norman said.

"Troy, I'll be fine. Fall back and I'll be in touch."

Norman clapped. "Good. You're learning fast who's the master and who isn't."

One of the guards came in with a box of pizza. "Y'all hungry? We got pizza."

Norman opened the box and said, "Have some."

Sean passed. "I'm good."

"You sure? Because it's hot." Norman picked up a slice and took a bite. "Hmm, and tasty, too." He used the back of his hand to wipe the tomato sauce from the side of his mouth. "Hey, you guys want some of this?"

"Naw, we got our own out there. We'll be back."

"After we eat, we can make our move," Norman directed before the two guards left him and Sean alone.

"You're going to be hungry. I suggest you take at least one slice. No telling when we'll get a chance to eat . . ."

Before he could finish saying the word "again," Norman's head wobbled and then he was out.

Sean said, "What in the world?"

He reached forward and barely touched Norman. Norman's head fell on the table. The door flew open. Sean saw something he wished he hadn't. He caught a glimpse of the silhouette of the woman who held his heart standing in front of Savannah. Where was Troy? Why didn't he stop them from entering this dungeon of death? But enough questions. He had to get the suitcase away from Norman and get those ladies out of there before whatever they used to knock Norman out wore off.

~ 25 ~

Seeing Sean fully awake was a sign of relief for Montana, because it would have been a struggle for her and Savannah to drag him out, but they were prepared to do so.

"Sean, you're okay," Montana said as she ran past Savannah and into his arms.

"Baby, what are you doing here? There are more guards."

"They all ate the pizza and are passed out but we're not sure for how long," Montana said.

"Let me get this case and then we need to get out of here."

"We took the weapons from them. The ones we saw anyway," Savannah said as she kept a lookout from the door to make sure they were all still out.

Sean picked up the silver briefcase and searched Norman's pockets. He removed a cell phone and ordered, "Come on, ladies, let's go."

Savannah handed Sean one of the guard's guns. He led them out. Savannah allowed Montana to be in the middle as she covered the rear. The front door swung open. Asia was on the other side. "Come on, the car's waiting. I heard what was going on and drove back up. That drug will be wearing off soon, so we need to get to moving," Asia said.

Sean hopped in the driver seat and Montana hopped in the passenger seat, while Savannah and Asia got in the back seat. Sean hightailed it out of there. "Get Troy on the line now. I'll deal with y'all later," he said as he handed her his phone.

Troy answered on the first ring. "Man, what happened in there? Everything went black and then we didn't have any audio."

"Blake sisters."

"What? Savannah!" Troy yelled from the speaker phone.

"Troy, we'll talk later," Savannah said, apologetic.

Sean said, "We'll talk about all of this later, but for now I need for you to get the men in there and hold them down. I don't want to chance them coming to and risking the ladies' lives."

"Already in motion," Troy said. "I'm minutes from there. Get the ladies in a safe place and I'll let you know when the mess has been cleaned up."

Troy ended the call. Sean continued to drive farther from the warehouse. He spotted some of his men going in the opposite direction. Montana remained quiet. She was relieved to have Sean there with her, but she knew that now she and Savannah had switched places. She hoped Troy came out of it alive, or guilt would haunt her for the rest of her life.

Montana tried to pretend like she didn't see the frown on Sean's face. "Ladies, I appreciate what you did, but you don't realize the danger you all placed yourselves in. You could have been killed."

Montana reached over and touched his right hand. "I couldn't sit back and not do anything."

"How did y'all get in there anyway, and whose bright idea was it?"

Montana cleared her throat. "Sort of mine." Montana went on and told him how they were able to get inside.

Sean chuckled. "I tell you, ladies, you were born to do this. That was smart. I have to hand it to you all, but things could have backfired."

"It's the risk we were willing to take," Savannah said.

"This time it worked in you guys' favor. Let there not be a next time."

Neither Montana nor her sisters could make that type of promise. With life, you never knew what situation would come up. Montana knew in her heart when it came to protecting her sisters and someone she loved, she would do almost anything; even if it meant risking her own life.

Montana shifted in her seat and looked at Sean as he continued to drive. "Sean, no, it might not have been the best thing for us to do but even you have to admit, from what you told Troy, if we hadn't there's no telling where you were headed to next. I'm your woman and you think I'm going to sit idly by and let someone harm you?"

"Can you repeat the 'I'm your woman' part?" Sean smiled for the second time since seeing Montana's face. He squeezed her hand. "Montana, I was relieved to see your face, but scared that one of the guards, or even Norman would awaken and do you harm."

"I'm fine." Montana looked back at her sisters. "We're all fine."

"I know that. I got to get this to the FBI lab so, you ladies, stay in the car. Promise me," Sean said.

This time, Montana didn't cross any fingers. "Promise."

Once Sean was out of the car and inside of the Federal Building, Montana let out a huge sigh. "I didn't even have a chance to think about how scared I was. I didn't know you had sprinkled stuff on the pizza," Montana said.

Asia responded, "It was something I thought of at the last minute."

"Where did you get the stuff?" Savannah asked.

"Mike left his bag at your house. I was going to give it to him the next time I saw him."

"So in other words, you were snooping and came across it," Montana said.

"Not really snooping. Just making sure there wasn't something in there he was going to need right away." Asia pulled out the brown bottle and showed it to Montana and Savannah.

Savannah opened the top of the box and saw what looked like a regular pizza. "So how did you know it would knock them out?"

"You can find out a lot of stuff on the Internet," Asia responded.

Savannah's phone rang. "No, Troy, he just left to go into the FBI building. Okay. I'll have Montana tell him. Montana, Norman has a plant in the FBI. You need to get to Sean before he makes the transfer."

Montana dialed Sean's number, but the call went straight to voice mail. Montana said, "I'm going in. Call Troy back and ask him who he would be going to see."

Savannah got Troy on the line and put him on speaker. "Troy, thanks. Montana's going to go in and see if she can get to him because he's still not answering his phone."

"Normally, I would not agree but it's imperative that they do not get those vials until we can determine which one is the mole," Troy said from the other end of the phone.

Montana double-checked her purse to make sure she had her identification just in case she needed it.

She exited the car to go look for her man.

26

Sean tapped his feet as he waited in the long line to go through the security terminal. His phone wasn't working so he couldn't call the agents he was there to see. He would ask one of the guards to call when it was his turn.

He wasn't too sure the vials would clear the conveyor belt. He didn't want them to think he was a terrorist so he would be sure to make known his presence and why he was there. "Finally," he said out loud when his turn came up. "It's important that I see Agent Sleeves. He's not expecting me, but can you call him and tell him that Sean Patterson is here with some important information on the case we've been working on?" Sean handed the guard his identification that gave him top government clearance.

Sean walked behind the guard through the security gate.

"Sean. Sean!" he heard Montana yell.

He turned in the direction of her voice and saw her running past the other people. Sean was livid. She was bringing too much attention to herself and to him. After this was over, he would have to have a long talk with her. He motioned for the guard to stop. "That's my girlfriend. It must be urgent. I'll be right back."

Sean, while still carrying the silver suitcase, walked quickly and Montana continued to run toward him. They almost collided. "Montana, what's wrong with you?" Sean looked back at the guard, who was now watching him closely.

"Troy called. There's a mole. He said do not make the transfer. I had to stop you before you did."

"Come with me. I need to get this upstairs."

"Did you not hear anything I said? You can't hand this over. One of the agents is a mole and works with that Norman guy."

"Are you sure?" Sean asked.

"I'm not but Troy must be if he sent me in here to get you."

"Look. Take this." Sean handed Montana the silver case. "Go directly back to the car. If I'm not there five minutes after you, then haul tail out of here and we'll catch up later."

"But, Sean—"

He interrupted her. "Montana, do as I say. I don't have time to discuss this with you." Sean watched Montana leave and he headed back to where the guard stood. "Change of plans. I'll just call him and come back another time."

"Are you sure? I radioed and told him you were here, so he's expecting you," the guard stated.

"My girlfriend's sister got hurt in an accident so I need to rush to the hospital."

"Sorry to hear that. I'll call him and tell him," the guard said.

"Thank you. Thank you very much."

Sean walked away but not without feeling like he was being watched. He turned around and didn't see anything or anyone who looked out of the ordinary. He walked briskly out to the car. Sean opened the door, but only saw two sets of eyes staring back at him.

Savannah said, "Whew. Glad you're here, but where's Montana? She went looking for you."

"Did she come looking for me after she came back with the silver suitcase?" he asked.

"No. She went looking for you after Troy said there's a mole," Asia responded.

Sean cursed and hit the steering wheel. Just then a dark blue car whipped by him. He jumped behind the wheel. "Buckle up, ladies. He has Montana."

"Nooo," Savannah screamed as Sean started up the car and swung it in reverse. He didn't wait for the bar to fly up to let him out. He mashed on the gas and ran right through it as little pieces of the bar flew up in the air.

Sean didn't have to tell Savannah what to do. While he chased the car, she called Troy to inform him of what had transpired.

"I shouldn't have sent her back by herself," Sean said.

Asia said, "Sean, I hope she remembers she still has a gun strapped to her ankle."

"I hope so too, because the guy who has her will not hesitate to kill her."

Savannah said, "Troy had the plate run. It belongs to an Agent Nelson."

Sean shouted, "Tell Troy where we are. I might need some reinforcements."

Savannah put Troy's call on speaker. "I'm going to try. Most of our men have been cleaning up the warehouse situation."

"Tell me you got him," Sean said as the adrenaline continued to run through his body. He dodged in and out of traffic to keep up with Nelson's car.

"We did, but he's not talking."

"How did you find out about Nelson?" Sean asked.

"One of the guards snitched."

Sean slammed on his brakes. He came inches away from slamming into the back of an eighteen-wheeler. Sweat dripped from his forehead as the car swerved, landing in the next lane. He glanced in the back seat to make sure Savannah and Asia were okay. He pulled safely back into traffic and zipped in and out of lanes until he was able to locate Nelson's car.

Sean revved up the engine and got right on Nelson's tail. The front of Savannah's car touched the back of Nelson's. "I'm about to go around. I need for you to tell me if you can see Montana in the front or back seat," he yelled out to Montana's sisters.

He jumped in the left lane and now his and Nelson's cars were side by side.

"I can't see anything, the windows are too dark," Asia yelled.

"Don't worry. He is not going to get away," Sean assured them.

27

Montana rubbed the back of her head. It felt like someone was hitting it with a hammer. She felt in a daze. All she could see when she opened her eyes was darkness. Once her eyes adjusted, she noticed she was surrounded by brooms and mops and what looked like cleaning supplies. *Where am I?* she asked herself. She blinked her eyes a few times and everything became clear.

She recalled stopping Sean and then heading back toward the car where her sisters waited. She looked down now and noticed the silver briefcase she'd had wasn't with her. She reached for the door and to her surprise it wasn't locked, but something must have been behind it because it wouldn't open. She used all of the strength she had and used her shoulders and body to push it open. She almost slipped and fell on the floor of the garage.

She ran out to where the car had been parked. They were nowhere in sight. She reached in her pocket but didn't realize she didn't have her cell phone until then. Someone had attacked her and taken the briefcase.

Montana had to reach Sean and her sisters. She knew they were probably wondering her whereabouts by now. Instead of going back into the Federal Building, she walked to the building next door. She got attacked there, so she didn't trust anyone in that building. She would take her chances.

The front door glided open when she walked up. The security guard asked, "Ma'am, may I help you?"

"Yes. I was attacked and I need to use your phone."

"Oh my goodness. Did you see your attacker?"

"No. They got away with everything," she responded.

The guard picked up the phone. "I'll get the police here."

"I just need to speak with my boyfriend. He's a cop," she partially lied.

"Sure. Have a seat," the guard said. He was very accommodating. "I better lock the front door just in case your attacker saw you come over here."

"Good idea," Montana said as she dialed Savannah's number because she didn't know

Sean's number by heart. She kept one eye on the door just in case she saw someone in a suit come that way. She tapped her foot. Savannah didn't answer. She dialed Asia's number.

Asia answered.

"Asia, it's me."

Asia screamed. "Can he hear you?"

"Nobody can hear me but the security guard. Where are y'all?"

"We're right behind you," Asia said.

Montana turned around but didn't see anyone. "I don't see y'all."

"Well, don't raise your head. We don't want him to do anything to you."

"Uh, I think there's been a mix-up. I'm at a building right next to the Federal Building."

Asia screamed in her ear again. The next voice she heard was Sean's. "Baby, we thought you were abducted."

Montana's rubbed the knot on the back of her head. "I got knocked out. Somebody got the vials."

"We know. We're behind them now. We thought you were in the car with him."

"Don't worry about me right now. Get those vials. I'll catch a taxi home."

"Negative. I'm sending Mike to get you. Do not leave with anyone else but Mike."

Montana assured Sean she wouldn't. She faced the security guard. "Thanks for letting me use the phone. Do you mind if I wait here until my ride comes?"

"No, but are you sure you don't want me to call the police?" he asked, showing concern.

"My boyfriend's going to handle it. He's sending his friend to pick me up. If I'm lucky, he'll catch who did this to me."

"I hope they do. It's a shame people can't go anywhere without the threat of being attacked," the security guard said.

Montana pretended to be interested in what the security guard had to say, as the retired ex-military man went on and on about things he had seen in his sixty-some years of living. He said Montana reminded him of one of his estranged daughters. She encouraged him to reach out to her. "Time heals all wounds. Maybe she'll realize what happened between you and her mother didn't have anything to do with her."

The misty-eyed security guard tried to hide his weeping eyes. "Look, I'm going to make me some coffee. You want a cup?"

"No. I don't want anything but my bed right now." Montana's hand automatically went back to her aching head.

"Maybe you should get that checked out."

Montana was glad that the security guard left her alone. She needed to get her thoughts together. How could she have not seen the person come for her? She should have been more aware of her surroundings. She was just concerned with getting back to the car with the vials. She played the moments leading up to the attack again in her head. She recalled feeling like she was being followed but when she turned around she didn't see anyone. Just when she was about to round the corner to where her sisters waited, that's when the attacker made his move.

Mike's face appeared through the glass of the door. She mouthed, "Will open as soon as the guard gets back."

Mike shook his head to let her know he understood. The guard returned carrying a hot cup of coffee.

"That's my ride. Thanks for all of your help."

The guard placed the cup of coffee down on the desk, pulled the keys from his waistband, and went and unlocked the door.

Mike walked in. Montana walked up to him and hugged him. "I'm so glad to see you."

"I'm just glad you're okay," Mike responded.

Montana said, "This guy here helped keep me safe."

Mike shook his hand. "Thanks, man."

"Get this lady some medical help. Ma'am, I hope your boyfriend catches who did this to you."

"Me too," Montana said, and she followed Mike to his car.

~ 28 ~

"He is determined not to stop," Savannah yelled.

"Which one of you is a good shot?" Sean asked.

"Me," Savannah and Asia said in unison.

Sean couldn't do anything but chuckle. "Well, ladies, you're about to try out your marksman skills. I need you to shoot out his tires."

Sean rushed to the side of Nelson's car. He rolled down the windows.

Nelson increased his speed.

Sean increased his. "Now," he yelled.

He wasn't sure which one shot, but the air in Nelson's car tires deflated and Nelson started losing control of his car. The car almost came into Sean's lane. Sean sped up and he saw Nelson's car hit the median. Sparks could be seen. Sean eased the car over and stopped it. "Savannah, get behind the wheel and be prepared to speed off when I get back."

Sean jumped from behind the wheel and ran back to where Nelson was. Nelson's bloody head was on the steering wheel.

A concerned motorist stopped. "I called nine-one-one. Someone's on their way," he said.

Sean responded, "Good." He held out his government badge. At a quick glance, it looked like he was law enforcement. "I got this," Sean insisted. He saw his men come in what appeared to be a real ambulance.

"Fellows, I think he's dead, but check to be sure," Sean said.

The concerned motorist gasped. "Do y'all need my statement?"

"No, sir. I witnessed it so I got all the authorities need."

He handed Sean a business card. "If you need me, I can be reached at that number."

Sean patted him on the shoulder. "Thanks for being a concerned citizen. The state of Texas thanks you."

The motorist reluctantly got back in his car.

Sean made sure the motorist was gone before he barked out orders. "Hand me that briefcase."

As soon as Sean had the silver briefcase, he left the team to do what they knew how to do best: clean up. He jumped in the passenger seat of the car and told Savannah, "Drive."

"Where to?"

"Back to your place . . . well, Montana's."

Less than forty-five minutes later they were reunited. The sisters couldn't stop hugging each other. Sean checked Montana's head out and saw a knot and assumed it was probably a concussion. He placed an icepack on the spot where she had been hit.

Savannah handed Montana two ibuprofen pills and a bottle of water. Montana took the pills and handed the bottle to Sean.

"You ladies can go downstairs if you like. I'll make sure she's okay."

"I'm fine. I'm not a baby, okay?" Montana protested. She took control and held on to the icepack.

Savannah and Asia left Sean and Montana alone.

"You're so stubborn, but I love you anyway," Sean said as he bent down and kissed Montana.

Sean's and Montana's bodies leaned backward. "Ouch," she said.

Sean got up. "Baby, I'm sorry. I got carried away."

"It's not entirely your fault. All I've been thinking about since we reunited is to taste your lips on mine," Montana confessed.

"Troy is on his way over, so as soon as he gets here we'll be leaving to take these vials to a secure place. I won't be able to rest until we've destroyed them." Sean glanced at the silver briefcase that now sat on the other side of Montana's bed.

"It must be something that is worth a federal agent risking his job and life for."

"Greed will eat a man alive if he lets it," Sean said.

"For sure. All of this excitement has me sleepy," Montana said.

"Lie down. Now don't get mad because if it's a concussion, I can't let you sleep long," Sean said.

Montana closed her eyes and it wasn't long afterward when she fell asleep.

Asia brought Sean her iPad. He used it to log in to his private server so he could find out more information about Agent Nelson. A light knock was heard on Montana's door.

Sean got up and saw Troy on the other side. "Give me a minute and I'll meet you downstairs," Sean said.

He shook Montana. She sleepily acknowledged him. "I'm okay. Can I go back to sleep now?"

"Sure. I'll send one of your sisters up to watch you. Troy's here. I'll be back as soon as I can. Okay, sweetheart?"

"You're my hero," Montana said.

Sean kissed her on the forehead. "No, baby, you're my hero. If you wouldn't have saved me from Norman, I would probably be dead by now."

Sean grabbed the silver briefcase and left to meet Troy downstairs.

He and Savannah were in a heated discussion. Sean cleared his throat. "Man, I'm ready. Savannah, I told Montana one of y'all would be up to check on her. Make sure you wake her up periodically."

Savannah pouted, but said, "We got this. Y'all just do what y'all got to do."

Sean didn't know what had transpired between her and Troy but he didn't have time to find out. He followed Troy out the front door so they could go dispose of the vials.

~ 29 ~

Montana woke up the next day fully alert. She was no longer feeling any pain. After Savannah and Asia took turns waking her up through the night, she was still able to get some much-needed rest. When she woke up around eight Savannah and Asia were both asleep in her room; one on the chaise, and one on the other side of her bed. She let them sleep.

She showered, dressed, and then headed downstairs to cook breakfast. The doorbell rang just as she neared the bottom of the stairs. She looked through the peephole. She didn't recognize one of the men, but sighed when she saw the other guy was Jason.

She opened the door. "Jason, come on in. I was just about to cook breakfast."

"Is Sean here?" Jason asked.

"No. Have you tried him on his cell?" Montana asked as she held the door open.

"Yes. Well, tell him to call me when you talk to him," Jason said.

The guy standing next to him never said a word.

"Okay. Are you sure you don't want anything?" Montana said. "It'll be about thirty to an hour, but you're welcome to stay and have breakfast with us."

"No. We got work to do, but thanks anyway," Jason responded.

Montana closed her door and locked it. She looked out the peephole and noticed Jason get in the driver side and the other guy get in the passenger side. She located her cell phone and called Sean.

"Call Jason. Something doesn't seem right with him," she said on the voice mail she left since Sean didn't answer his phone.

The knot on the back of Montana's head had gone down and she didn't feel any pain. She wondered what was going on with the vials. Pushing all of that out of her mind, she went to the kitchen and cooked a hearty breakfast, just in case Sean and Troy stopped by.

Savannah was the first one to come downstairs. They greeted each other with a hug. "Sis, we were worried about you," Savannah said as she fixed her a plate.

"I'm fine. Thank God," Montana said, wiping the lone tear threatening to fall from her cheek.

"Troy's not answering his phone. I was a little harsh with him. Now I'm feeling bad about it," Savannah said in between bites.

"What was the argument about?" Montana asked as she took a seat at the kitchen table with a plate of food.

"He was upset that we endangered our lives by going to Fort Worth. I told him that the last I checked, he wasn't my daddy. That I was a grown woman and could do whatever I wanted, whenever I wanted, and if he didn't like it, he could step."

"Ouch," Montana said as she sipped some of her juice.

"I know what he was saying but I just felt like he was a little too harsh with me so I bit back."

"He cares about you. You've been through a lot and he doesn't want to lose you. Give him some slack, sis. Or is there more going on here than you're telling me?" Montana asked.

Savannah stared at her plate. "I'm afraid. There, I said it."

"Not you. You're a bad chick. Thanks to you, I got my man back." Montana tried to lighten up the situation.

"I'm afraid that Troy will get an assignment and it might take him away from me permanently. Like Dad. I don't know if I could deal with losing another man I love. And, Montana. I love Troy just as much as I love you and Asia, if not more."

"Wow," Montana said at Savannah's revelation.

"I know it's stupid of me to say things to push him away, but I got to get my feelings in check. I feel like I'm losing control. Now he's not answering my calls. I don't know what to do." Savannah threw her hands up in the air.

Montana wasn't used to seeing Savannah like this. She was the older sister who usually had everything under control, or at least she always seemed to have it under control. "I'm going to tell you what Dad used to tell me about situations. Pray about it."

"I know. I'm just being stubborn," Savannah responded.

The house phone rang. Montana got up and answered. She held the phone out. "It's for you."

Savannah eased up from behind the table and took the phone.

Montana left the kitchen to give her some privacy. Troy was calling Savannah, so why hadn't she heard from Sean? She pulled out her cell phone to call him. She looked at his name in her saved contacts. Maybe she had misread Sean. She was under the impression they were getting closer. If Sean wanted to talk, he would have to call her. She opted not to call. She threw the cell phone on the sofa.

Savannah came in the living room shortly thereafter. "All's forgiven. We've made up," she said with a smile on her face.

Montana wasn't feeling too good. "That's good." A frown remained on her face.

"What's wrong?" Savannah asked, still standing up.

"Just thinking about these last few days."

"Yeah, right. You're thinking about Sean. Well, Sean is knocked out. Troy said they'll meet up with us later and give us an update."

Montana felt relieved a little, but was still uneasy that she hadn't talked to him. She knew she was being selfish because after all of the things that had been going on, she knew Sean had to be physically and mentally exhausted.

"Thanks for telling me, sis. I was wondering."

"I went through that with Troy. Troy tells me Sean is the real deal. He's loyal to those he loves."

But does he truly love me? Montana asked herself.

~ 30 ~

Sean needed those few hours of sleep. Norman was now behind bars and hoped his lawyers wouldn't be able to get him off on bail. Surely, no judge would release him but stranger things had happened. His body and mind now felt rejuvenated. After thanking God that he was alive to see another day, he looked at his phone and saw several missed calls. He smiled when he saw Montana's number was one of them.

He checked his messages. "That's odd," Sean said after listening to Montana's message. He also saw he had several missed calls from Jason.

Sean dressed and went in search of Troy. Troy was watching sports when he entered the living room area. "Man, have you talked to Jason?"

"No. I saw he had been trying to reach me so I called his phone but I'm not getting any answer."

"Well, Montana said he stopped by there and something didn't seem right to her."

Troy pulled out his phone and dialed a number. He put it on speaker. "Mike, have you talked to Jason?"

"No, but got calls. I was knocked out so didn't hear the phone ringing."

"Why was he over at Montana's looking for me?" Sean asked.

"I don't know what's up with that. I'll track him down and get back to y'all," Mike said.

Troy ended the call. "Guess we'll know soon enough."

"My gut is saying we need to go to his place."

"Let me find my shoes and then I'll be ready to go," Troy responded.

Twenty minutes later they were pulling up to Jason's apartment. "I didn't see his car," Sean said, as he found a parking spot.

"Neither did I," Troy responded.

Sean knocked on the door. No answer. Troy called Jason's phone. Sean said, "Did you hear that? Call his number again."

Troy obeyed. He put his ear to the door and heard the phone ringing. Sean put on some gloves and turned the doorknob so as not to destroy any fingerprints that may be there just in case there was foul play. The door didn't budge.

Troy said, "I got it." Troy pulled out a small, slim metal device. He used it to pick the lock. He turned the doorknob and it opened.

Jason's apartment was ransacked, but nothing was taken. Troy and Sean both had their guns out as they went from room to room.

Sean said, "Found him."

Troy walked in the bathroom behind him.

A note was taped to Jason's bloody body. Troy ripped the note away and read it. He handed it to Sean. "It's meant for you."

Sean read the note: "We're coming for you and anybody who knows you."

Sean dropped the note on the floor, but Troy bent down and picked it up and put in his pocket. "I better call this in," Troy said.

"I need to check on something."

While Troy was calling his friend, and the police department, Sean dialed Montana's number. "Baby, sorry I'm just calling. How are you feeling this morning?" he asked. He hoped she couldn't pick up on his nervousness.

"I'm doing fine. No headaches and I'm not dizzy anymore."

"That's good. Has anyone else stopped by there?"

"No. Did you ever catch up with Jason?" she asked.

"Sort of. I'll tell you about it when I get there. In the meantime, do not and I repeat do not answer the door for anyone."

When the police officers got there, they asked Troy and Sean many questions. Sean kept looking at his watch because he needed to get to Montana. Mike was doing his best to track Jason's car. The person who had it was more than likely Jason's killer. Mike sent a text message to both of their phones to indicate he had located the car.

Sean texted Mike back to let him know they would go check it out. As soon as the police were satisfied with their answers, they headed to Jupiter Road.

"He has to be the dumbest criminal," Troy said as they parked on the side of the road.

"Or it could be a setup," Sean responded. "Maybe we should get some reinforcements."

Troy gripped his weapon. "This is all the reinforcement we need."

"I got an uneasy feeling about this, man."

Just when they were getting ready to walk across the street, they noticed someone use a crowbar to break in Jason's car.

Troy shouted but the burglar looked back at Troy and then jumped in the car. As soon as the door closed, the car exploded.

Troy and Sean both hit the ground. Debris from the car flew and fell all over the place, barely missing Sean's truck.

Troy said, "Let's get out of here. We don't need to be here when the cops come."

People from some of the nearby buildings were coming out and checking their surroundings.

Troy called in the explosion as he and Sean drove in the opposite direction of it.

Sean called Montana. "Look. Something's come up. I need to pay Norman a visit."

Montana seemed disappointed but she didn't say anything. Sean ended the call as he drove to the federal prison where Norman was being held. After going through security, and after the guards verified his and Troy's security clearances, they were allowed through the gates.

"Patterson. Sean Patterson," the guard called his name over the intercom.

Sean walked up to the guard station. "I'm Sean."

"There seems to be a problem. I have here that the prisoner is being transferred to the Oklahoma facility."

"Who gave those orders?" Troy asked.

"I'm not at liberty to say," the guard responded.

Sean asked, "How long ago was this?"

The guard looked at the computer screen. "An hour ago."

Troy stated, "Let me speak to Colonel Payne."

"The colonel's off today," the guard responded.

Troy repeated himself. "I suggest you get the colonel on the phone, or some jobs might be in jeopardy."

Sean cursed under his breath. Norman was not supposed to be transferred. This was not good. Not good at all.

~ **31** ~

Montana ended up putting in the refrigerator the extra breakfast she had cooked. She called into the office to see how things were going. Fortunately for her, she was the boss, or she would have been fired.

Savannah and Asia were both busy doing their own thing. All of the sisters worked for themselves. They didn't all set out to do so, but it just happened that way. Montana smiled because if it weren't for her father's encouragement, she would still be spending countless hours slaving away making someone else richer. Instead, she used her contacts and her skills and started her own public relations firm. She had the nickname in the industry of the Image Maker, because even if her client was notorious, she could make him or her sound like the best thing since the television was invented.

Montana was good and the people she hired had to have that something extra special too.

Although she had a person over human resources, no one got hired without Montana's scrutiny and final approval.

Montana logged on to her office e-mail and followed up on several of her projects. Some of her regular clients needed press releases done for some upcoming events. She created bids for potential clients. She needed something to keep her mind occupied. Something to keep her mind off the events of the last few days. Something to keep her mind off Sean.

Montana was wrapped up in work when Savannah came downstairs. "Sean and Troy are pulling up outside."

Savannah went to the front door and opened it. She walked outside. Soon afterward, Sean walked in. He made his way directly to Montana. They held each other tight. He kissed her on the forehead before reaching for her hand. They walked to the sofa. Montana picked up the papers she had been working on and moved them and placed them on the coffee table in front of her.

"I've been so worried about you," Montana confessed.

"I might have to go to Oklahoma. Went to see Norman but he got transferred."

"Well, that's only about four hours away. I'll be okay."

"Another thing. Jason's dead."

Montana's hand flew to her mouth. "Oh my God. What happened?"

Sean stated what happened and told her about the explosion. "So, you see why I'm so concerned about your safety."

"My sisters are here, but now I'm wondering who the guy was with Sean. Let me do a quick sketch of him."

Montana got up and found a pen. She placed typing paper on the pad in front of her. She closed her eyes and drew the vision she saw in her head. The man had a round bald head. She opened her eyes and looked at the picture. "He was never introduced, but this is him."

Sean took the paper from Montana and looked at the picture. "Are you sure?" he asked.

"Positive. Does he work for you?"

"No, he's a federal agent."

Sean got up and left Montana alone. He returned, followed by Troy and Savannah. Sean's phone was glued to his ear.

When he got off the phone, he said, "Ladies, pack up some clothes. We need to get y'all to a safe house."

Montana protested, "We're fully capable of taking care of ourselves. I think our track record speaks for itself."

Montana saw fear in Sean's eyes. Something she'd never seen before. "I know you are. Just trust me on this. Please," Sean pled.

Montana turned her laptop off and placed it in the case.

Troy said, "Where's Asia?"

"She's at her place," Savannah responded.

Troy said, "We'll swing by and pick up Asia. Sean, we'll meet you and Montana at the safe house."

Montana was already on the phone with Asia. "Pack some bags. We're taking a trip."

Asia didn't ask questions. "Give me about thirty minutes."

Montana responded. "No, stay put. Troy and Savannah will call you when they're out front."

Sean helped Montana pack. Montana turned on the house alarm and the surveillance cameras. "Asia has it set where she can view what goes on here remotely."

"She's thought of everything, I see," Sean stated, sounding impressed.

"After Uncle Raymond tried to kill Savannah, we added extra security on top of what our dad already had in place."

"Troy needs to recruit you ladies because y'all some bad mamma jammas."

They both laughed as they entered Sean's car.

Sean said, "I need to swing by my place first and grab a few things."

Once they reached Sean's house, Montana decided she didn't want to remain behind. Sean's house wasn't as elaborate as Troy's but it was still nice. The one-story house was decorated in blacks and browns. Montana followed Sean through the rooms and she could think of many ways she could give his place a nice makeover.

Montana was staring at a picture of a woman and a man on the mantle when she felt Sean's arm wrap around her waist.

"That's a picture of my grandparents. It's the only picture I have."

"You look just like your grandfather," she said.

"Too bad I didn't get a chance to meet them before they died. That picture is the only thing that ties me to them," Sean said.

Montana turned around and wanted to remove the sadness she heard in Sean's voice. "If I have anything to do with it, you'll never be alone again."

Montana wasn't usually that forthcoming. She wrapped her arm around Sean's neck and pulled his lips on top of hers. She used her tongue and parted her lips to his welcoming mouth. The built-up passion didn't take long to ignite into a full-blown inferno.

Montana wrapped her legs around Sean's waist. Without breaking his lips away from her, Sean carried Montana to his bed. While he unbuckled his pants, Montana removed hers. Sean took control of removing her panties. He pushed her bra up and took each one of her nipples into his mouth, causing moans to seep out from both of them.

He used his free hand to open up her legs. His fingers inserted into her wet spot causing Montana's body to shiver. He removed his fingers and replaced them with his throbbing manhood. The moment he entered Montana's body, they both exhaled.

Montana wrapped her legs around his waist for a second time and enjoyed the ride. With each stroke, Sean was able to make Montana forget all of her worries. Time stood still as they became one with each other. If this was what pure bliss felt like, Montana didn't want it to ever end.

They both moaned, "I love you," as they climaxed.

~ 32 ~

Sean knew he shouldn't have made love to Montana because their lives could have been in danger, but he was feening for her and needed to feel the inside of her or he would have exploded within his pants and that wouldn't have been a nice sight. When she wrapped her legs around his waist, he lost all control and here they were now, lying naked in his bed like he had dreamed so many times.

The satisfied smile on her face made it all worth it. Montana was his dream come true and he would do whatever he needed to do to protect her. First order of business was getting dressed and getting her to the safe house.

Sean ran one of his hands through her hair. "Baby, as much as I would like to lie here with you, we need to get going."

"Okay. Where's your bathroom so I can freshen up?"

"Normally, I would be like, I'll meet you there. But you can use the one in here and I'll use the guest bathroom. I'll meet you in the living room when you finish."

Sean got up first. He extended his hand and helped her stand up out of the bed. He couldn't help admiring her round naked body. She had curves in all the right places and if she didn't take her fine self into the bathroom, he would lose all resolve again. "Go, you're too tempting," he blurted out.

Montana picked up her discarded clothes and went to the bathroom. Sean retrieved some clothes from his closet and went downstairs to wash up.

He beat Montana to the front door. He called out her name, but there was no answer. "Montana."

Still no answer.

Sean pulled out his gun and held it up as he eased through the hallway. He ran smack into Montana. "Ooh, Sean, you scared me."

Sean sighed. He placed his gun down to his side. "Montana, I thought something had happened to you."

"No. I probably didn't hear you because I had your fan on in the bathroom. I didn't want you to hear me. Well, let's just say I was taking care of business."

Sean blurted out laughing. "You're something else. Come on. I got everything I need."

Sean locked up his house and they headed to the designated safe house.

Troy, Asia, and Savannah were already there. He could tell by the curious looks they probably figured out they took a detour since it took them so long to get there.

Troy pulled Sean to the side. "I can tell from the magical glow you both have y'all were up to a little something something," Troy teased.

Sean ignored him. "Any news on Norman yet?"

"Let me make a few phone calls," Troy said.

Sean gave the sisters a tour of the safe house. "The panic room is located here so if someone intrudes while we're gone, just make it to this room."

Sean flipped the light on so they could see. He continued to say, "There's a staircase that winds around. Then if need be follow the tunnel and it'll take you to one of the nearby fields and there's a car there full of gas. The key is located by the door."

"Sean, man, come here," Troy yelled.

"Close this for me," Sean looked at Montana and said. Sean rushed to where Troy was standing.

Troy looked furious. "I just got a phone call. The convoy was attacked. Norman is back on the loose."

Sean clinched his fist. "This is what I was afraid was going to happen." Sean called Mike. "Mike, we're going to level five."

Troy stated, "When you want something done right, you do it yourself."

Sean's phone rang. The word "restricted" flashed across the screen. Norman's evil laugh sounded in his ear.

"You know you can't keep a good man down. Did you think you could keep me locked up? I'm a god in my world and my people will do whatever it takes. Did you find that note?"

"Norman, there's not a cave deep enough. If it takes me years, I will find you."

"One other thing. You might have all of the vials, but I still have the formula. My man will be making up another batch and this time, Mr. Patterson, you will not be able to stop us."

The phone went dead. Sean felt like throwing his phone across the room. "We got to catch this dude before he really goes through with this threat," Sean said.

Asia interrupted, "Why don't y'all concentrate on finding him and we"—Asia pointed to her two sisters and then to herself—"will look for the scientist he's using to make the stuff."

"No. I don't want any of you involved. You all need to stay out of it," Sean immediately disagreed.

"We need to work together on this. You two can't be all over the place," Savannah interjected.

Troy kept his mouth shut. Sean wanted to know why Troy wasn't backing him up on this. Sean looked at Montana. Montana looked away. "Troy, come on, man."

Troy rubbed his left eyebrow. "As much as I don't want my baby to be in harm's way, I'm confident that they can handle themselves."

"No. They just got lucky, man. Anything can happen. They are not equipped for battle," Sean protested.

Montana said, "Speak for yourself. We're prepared to do whatever it takes. If you feel we need more training, then train us; but I think me and my sisters are more than capable of handling this 'mad scientist.'"

Sean blurted out, "We don't have time for that."

Asia pushed her iPad in front of Sean. "I've been doing my own research trying to figure out where those vials could have been made. I've narrowed it down to several places. These are the three sites that he may have someone

working on it at. I need access to your database
so I can do some background checks on the
employees."

"Get with Mike and he'll get you all the access
you need," Troy stated.

Sean didn't want to cave in, but as more and
more of their men were getting killed, he reluctantly gave in and said, "You ladies handle the
scientist. Troy and I will go track down Norman.
We need to keep the lines of communication
open."

Troy added, "But instead of calling, text the
person, because either of us could be in a position where a ringing or vibrating phone could
interfere with our operations."

Sean said, "Everybody look at your watch. It's
sixteen hundred right now. Everybody got that."

All of the heads in the room acknowledged the
time. He continued, "Due to the nature of this,
someone from both sides will be in contact with
at least one person via text and inform the party
of what's going on. If trouble arises . . . type in
nine-one-one."

The sisters saluted Sean. Troy said, "You can
take my car. It's on full." Troy handed Savannah
his keys. "The red key is for this door." Troy
pulled Savannah in for a long kiss.

Sean, not wanting to feel left out, pulled Montana in for even a longer kiss.

Asia cleared her throat. "Hellooo. We got some criminals to catch, people."

Sean followed Troy out of the safe house in search of his nemesis, Norman.

Don't know if you're even close to anything in the other doors."

Montana shook her head. "No, Asia. I don't recall anything about a male. She had to initial those on her file." I found a print-out having to do with animal experimentation. Is it possible you could have taken the file for one?" she asked.

The guard said, "Well, Ms. Voslander, we're all...

~ 33 ~

Montana was having second thoughts about their plans on tracking down the scientist. "I don't know why I let you two talk me into this," she repeated over and over as they pulled up to one of the laboratories on Asia's list.

She did a quick glance of herself in the mirror. Her hair was pulled back into a bun and she had on some thick Coke-bottle glasses. She looked like a complete nerd.

"Those Coke bottles are cameras. We just need you to get in there and get a lay of the place for us," Asia said.

"Get in and get out," Montana said to herself as she walked up the walkway to the pharmaceutical building.

The guard stopped her. "Ma'am. I don't think I've seen you around before."

"I just started," Montana said. She pulled out the fake badge Asia had made. The guard scanned it. Montana held her breath until she heard the door click.

"Don't forget to enter your code to get through the other door."

Montana clenched her teeth; Asia hadn't said anything about a code. She had to think quick on her feet. "I forgot my notebook inside. It has all of that information. Is it possible you can enter the code for me?" she asked.

The guard said, "Well, Ms. Applegate, maybe you should wait until your supervisor is here because I'm really not supposed to do that."

Montana pulled out some fake tears. "But, this is my first day. I really need this job. My rent's overdue and if I don't have my rent in two weeks, I'm on the streets."

The guard felt sorry for Montana. "Calm down. I'll let you in this time, but remember, you must have your code the next time. So don't forget your folder."

Montana straightened up her face. "God bless you and I won't. I promise."

Montana watched the guard enter the code and filed it in her memory for future use, just in case. She used the badge to access other parts of the lab. She went to the location according to the layout that Asia had shown her but the lab area was empty. She looked around to see if there was any trace of anything.

"Miss, you're not supposed to be in here," an older man wearing a white lab smock said.

"I was looking for . . ." Montana couldn't recall the man's name. She was stuck.

"Braylon? Braylon got fired last week. We discovered he was using company equipment and time to work on his own private projects. That's not tolerated here."

"I went to school with Braylon. He's the one who told me about the job here," Montana lied.

"Well, we hated to lose him, but we have to trust our employees."

"Do you know how I can reach him? I really just wanted to thank him," Montana stated.

"What's your name?" the man asked.

"Ms. Applegate. Lisa Applegate."

"Well, Lisa, I wasn't aware we hired anyone new. I'm supposed to be notified of all new hires. But that's what happens when your company sells out to a bigger and larger corporation. I won't complain though. I still got a job in this bad economy."

Montana was shaking her head in agreement, hoping he would hurry up and give her the information she needed.

"Wait right here. I think I have it somewhere."

While he was gone to look for the information, Montana decided to skim through the things that were left in the lab. She picked up a yellow steno pad and slipped it in her pocket. She placed an empty used vial in one of the plastic bags and slipped it into her other pocket.

"Lisa," the scientist yelled out several times.

It took a moment for the name to register in Montana's head. "Oh, yes. I'm sorry, my mind was a million miles away."

"Well, young lady, when you're in the lab, you have to focus. Don't be letting your mind wander like that," he said, giving her a verbal reprimand.

"Oh, I won't."

"I wrote down his phone number for you. I have his address, but you'll have to get that from him." He handed her the yellow slip of paper.

"Oh, thank you. This is more than enough. I just wanted to call him anyway," Montana assured him. She slipped the paper into her white lab coat pocket.

"Well, I'm about to shut it down. If there's nothing else, you can follow me out."

"I need to use the bathroom first. I got a long ride home."

"Oh, I understand. Well, I'll see you tomorrow. Just flip that switch when you leave."

Montana detoured to the women's bathroom and pretended that she had to use it by staying in there as long as she thought it would normally take. She went through the motions of flushing the toilet and washing her hands.

When she exited the bathroom, the hallway was dark except for the light beaming from the office she needed to enter. She slipped in the room undetected. She went through the files and wrote down the name and number of the man they were looking for. Montana slipped back out of the room and rushed down the hallway at a fast pace. Her brisk walk was almost at a sprint as she flipped the light off and exited the building.

She smiled at the security guard as she walked by. He waved. She waved back. She tried to monitor her pace as she walked back to the car where Savannah and Asia waited.

Montana didn't exhale until she was safely in the passenger seat. She pulled out the yellow sticky note and handed it to Asia, who was sitting in the back. "Bingo."

"Yes." Asia grabbed it and then entered the name and number in her iPad. "Ladies, we're going to take a little trip to McKinney."

Savannah's eyes got big. "Sis, you can sit this one out, if you want," Montana said. "Asia and I can handle this."

Savannah shook her head. "No. I'm okay. I just had a flashback moment."

Montana knew what she meant. She had a flashback too.

Sean's pulse rate rose as he raced up the highway toward Oklahoma. They were trying to get in the area before nightfall. Norman wasn't stupid enough to stay out in the wide open. He had been worried about the ladies but Savannah had checked in with Troy so that eased some of his concern.

Troy said, "I think that's them."

"Where?" Sean asked.

Troy pointed in the opposite direction. Sean had to try not to bring attention to themselves so he couldn't whip his vehicle around via the center lane like he wanted. Instead he sped up and got off on the next exit and did a U-turn. He sped up in traffic until he was a few cars behind.

"We got positive ID," Troy told Mike while Sean made sure he stayed a good distance away. "We're on 35 heading south. We're about thirty miles from the Texas-Oklahoma state line."

"Check this out, Troy," Sean said.

Another vehicle with dark-tinted windows sped past them and then jumped behind the vehicle they were following.

"I wonder if he was in that one," Troy said.

"He's in one of them. Either way, we're going to locate Norman. Norman is not getting out of my sight."

Troy's phone alerted him to another text message. "That's Vanna. She wants me to call her if I can." Troy dialed Savannah's number. "Baby, what's up?"

"We got positive ID on the guy who created those vials. He's no longer working at the company. They fired him last week. Asia's tracked down where he lives but, before proceeding, I wanted to let you know what's going on."

Sean was glad to see that they both were successful at locating their suspects but apprehending both could be deadly. "Proceed with caution," he said. "Since he knows how to make biological chemical weapons, there's no telling what trick he will use if he feels threatened."

Savannah responded, "Montana's working on our disguises now. Don't worry. We're going in as a team. Asia's the lookout. We'll check in right before we start the next phase of our operation."

"Sounds like a plan," Troy said. They ended the call.

Sean thought out loud, "I hope they aren't biting off more than they can chew."

Troy responded, "My girl's bad. She can handle herself. Montana's no joke either. Let's let the ladies do their thing and we'll do ours. Come on, man, I need you to focus on this one hundred percent."

Sean knew Troy was right. He couldn't afford to think about what Montana was doing. One mistake and Norman would be lost, or worse, other people could lose their lives. They were now reentering Texas.

"Are our men in place? That roadblock shouldn't be too far ahead," Sean said.

Troy confirmed with Mike that everything was set. "Slow down, man. We should be coming up on it."

Just as Troy predicted, the roadblock had cars slowing down. Troy got in the left lane, however, and jumped back in the right lane so he would only be one car length away from Norman and his convoy.

"There go the boys in blue," Sean said. "Hope this works."

Mike said over the speaker phone. "They are doing random checks. I gave them the description of the two vehicles Troy described so they should be stopped here shortly."

"Bingo. It's time, fellows," Troy said.

The cars came to a complete stop. Sean pulled over slightly on the shoulder. One of the officers walked back to his car. "Sir, we're going to have to ask you to get out of the car." The state trooper looked at Troy. "And you too, sir."

Neither Troy or Sean moved.

"How did I do? Y'all like my Texas accent?" Franklin asked as he pretended to be interrogating them.

"What's the 411?" Sean asked.

"Confirmed Norman is in the lead car. We're holding them as long as we can. How do you think we should proceed?"

"Make sure the one Norman is in has a flat tire and we'll take it from here."

"Yes, sir. Sir, you two can get back in your vehicle now."

Sean and Troy smiled and pretended to do as directed.

Once Franklin carried out the order to stick something in the tire of the car Norman was in, Sean drove slowly behind and watched as the car wobbled a little before pulling over to the side of the road.

The traffic was stopped so that if any weapons were fired, hopefully no one would get hurt.

Sean and Troy eased out of their cars, ready to fire their weapons as their men ambushed both vehicles and pulled out everyone in the cars without incident.

Norman and Sean's eyes locked. "So we meet again," Norman said as a sinister smile crossed his face.

"This time, I'm going to make sure you stay locked up," Sean said as he pulled Norman's arms behind his back and placed the handcuffs around his wrist.

"Ouch. You don't want me to sue you for mishandling of a prisoner, do you?"

"You're a fugitive so I'm sure no one cares," Sean responded.

"I almost got away with it but I underestimated you, Sean Patterson."

"That you did."

Sean wasn't concerned about the other prisoners. He pushed Norman through the barricade. Troy opened up the back door. Sean pushed Norman's head down while pushing him in the back. Troy said, "I'll sit with him. He might try to get some ideas." Troy slid in the back of the car next to Norman.

"You want to talk bad now but you wasn't talking so bad when we were beating your ass now were you?" Norman sneered.

"Sean, hurry up and get us to Dallas before I save the taxpayers' money," Troy said.

Sean looked in the rearview mirror. He knew what Troy meant. It was taking everything within him not to press his semiautomatic weapon to Norman's dome and pull the trigger.

He imagined doing so and smiled.

Norman was looking at him in the rearview mirror but his smile faded when he saw Sean's smile.

Sean said to himself, *Checkmate*.

~ 35 ~

Montana and Savannah made sure they were properly equipped with weapons, mace, and cell phones.

"I feel like Nicki Minaj in this disguise," Savannah said as she glanced at herself in the full-length mirror.

"I did do a good job, didn't I?" Montana laughed.

"I'm like the perfect clay, can be molded into perfection," Savannah said with confidence.

Both sisters laughed.

Asia peeped her head in the doorway. "Hot mamas. Y'all ready for phase two?"

Montana shifted her garter. "Let's do this."

Montana locked up her house and reactivated the alarm.

She hopped in the front passenger seat of Savannah's car and they rode to Braylon's apartment in McKinney.

Asia said, "This shouldn't be too hard, but I still don't want you to take any unnecessary chances. He looks like a geek, but he's a freaky geek."

"I can't believe he thought he won private dancers," Montana said as she applied a coat of lip gloss so her lips could shimmer. She puckered up.

"Fortunately for me, it was easy to hack into his computer so I could see what he did when he wasn't creating killing formula," Asia said.

Savannah said, "I hope this doesn't take too long. This thing is about to cut off my circulation." She adjusted the corset.

Asia pulled the car up in the subdivision. "I got the monitor on. If you need backup, don't hesitate to let me know."

Montana smacked her lips. "We got this, little sis. You just handle your end."

"Oh, you bad now, huh," Asia teased.

"Yes, I'm a bad mamma jamma," Montana responded.

"Shut your mouth." Savannah burst out laughing.

Montana got out of the car. Savannah got out of the car with the duffle bag filled with some items they were going to need.

Dressed in trench coats and sexy gear, they walked up to Braylon's house. Montana knocked several times.

Braylon was not as tall as Montana expected. He was several inches shorter than her. His blond curly hair hung down to his shoulders. Montana's flesh crawled when his creepy smile showed two buck teeth.

"Ladies, I'm so excited, it's hard for me to contain myself." Braylon opened the door wider as Montana and Savannah walked in. He clicked the lock and used a key to lock another lock.

Montana looked at Savannah and Savannah looked at her, raising an eyebrow.

Savannah said, "Where do you want us to set up for your private show?"

"Follow me, you chocolate beauties." Braylon salivated at the mouth as he led them down the hall to a room. "Can I help you with anything?"

"You sure can. Plug this up for me," Savannah said as she pulled out a small CD player.

Braylon eagerly did it. He sat down on the sofa.

"Oh, no, big boy. I need you in a chair," Montana said seductively.

Braylon left the room and returned with a brown chair. He took a seat.

Savannah pulled out some chocolate-covered strawberries. She was bending over. When she looked back he was checking out her position. "You do like strawberries, don't you?" she asked.

He licked his lips. "Yes. Just as much as I love chocolate."

Montana felt the hairs on the back of her neck rise. The music started playing. Montana imagined she was a video girl and started swaying her hips to the mid-tempo beat. She removed her coat and she stood in a Playboy Bunny outfit minus the ears.

Braylon was foaming at the mouth. Montana took the scarf from around her neck and then played with it by using it on his body. He reached out to touch her. Montana said, "No, big boy. No touching. Well, not yet anyway."

"Please," he begged.

Savannah walked up carrying two ropes. "Since you can't obey, I'm going have to tie you up."

"Ooh, please do," he responded with lust-filled eyes.

Savannah tied one of his hands to one arm of the chair, while Montana tied his other hand to the other side of the chair. Montana danced and moved behind him so he couldn't see her, but he wasn't paying attention to her at this point because Savannah was putting on a show.

She did a seductive move that had Braylon gasping.

While Savannah had his full attention, Montana slipped down the hall. She went from room to room, but found nothing. She tried to open up one door and it wouldn't budge. "Finally," she said out loud.

Montana went back to where Braylon and Savannah were. She playfully moved Savannah out of the way. She bent down in front of Braylon and did a move where his eyes were not bucked. She reached for his belt loop and eased his pants off.

She winked at Savannah. Savannah didn't need any words. While Montana kept Braylon occupied with her seductive moves, Savannah located his keys and eased them out of his pants pocket and placed them softly on the sofa.

"Don't move, big boy. I need to tell Monet something."

Braylon was like silly putty in Montana's hands. Montana walked over to Savannah and whispered in her ear. Montana picked up the chocolate-coated strawberries and dipped them in a white powdery substance, as Savannah eased out of the room.

Montana licked her lips. "Let me feed you this and then I got something else you can eat."

"Mmm hmm. I can't wait," Braylon stated.

"Open wide," she said.

Braylon opened his mouth up. Montana teased him with the strawberry and then allowed him to eat it as the juices slid around his mouth.

"Have another one. They are so juicy. You can't have just one." Montana gripped one of her breasts for effect.

Braylan foamed at the mouth as she placed another coated strawberry in his mouth. His eyes glazed over. He was oblivious to everything that was going on. At least Montana hoped so.

She was relieved when Savannah returned to the room. She signaled that it was time for them to go.

Montana ignored the painful look in Braylan's face when he realized what was happening. He was just paralyzed and couldn't do anything about it. She inserted the syringe in his thigh and the medicine took immediate effect. Braylon was knocked completely out.

Montana gathered up all of their items and placed them back in the duffle bag. Savannah fumbled with the front door until she finally found the key.

By the time they made it out, Mike and some other guy were pulled up behind Savannah's car.

Mike said, "Ladies, good job. We got it from here."

"Just like a man. Wanting to take credit after the woman has done all of the work," Asia stated.

Mike blew her a kiss. Asia threw him the finger.

Savannah said, "You might need this."

Savannah threw Mike Braylon's keys.

Montana sighed as she slipped into the passenger seat. She thanked God for their successful mission.

~ 36 ~

Sean clicked his phone off and looked in the rearview mirror. "Operation Save Dallas Water Supply is a wrap. All parties have been apprehended."

Norman looked up at the rearview mirror. "Just because you have me doesn't mean the plan isn't going to be executed."

"It is my pleasure to tell you that your scientist is at this time incapacitated and the only thing he will be seeing is a jail cell, just like you, my friend."

Rage filled Norman's eyes. "I don't believe it."

"You do know someone named Braylon, don't you?" Sean asked.

"Not a hair on Braylon's head had better be harmed," Norman said.

Troy said, "Right now you need to be concerned about yourself."

"Oh, you can't touch me."

"No, we're not going to do anything. We're just going to make sure you never see the light of day again. By the time it's all over, you're going to wish I would have killed you," Sean said.

"I'm not going out without a fight." Norman started kicking the seat.

Troy did his best to control him but Norman head-butted him.

Sean whipped the car over to the curb so fast. He stopped the car, jumped from behind the wheel, and went to the right side of the car. He pulled Norman out, hitting his head on the top of the car. The rage Sean had been holding since Troy had been abducted released in the punches he delivered to Norman's body.

"You tried to kill my best friend and my woman, do you know what I could do to you?" he said as he hit Norman over and over.

What was sure to be a deadly blow was blocked by Troy grabbing Sean's arm. "Man, he's not worth it."

Sean released the grip he had on Norman and his limp body fell to the ground.

Troy picked Norman up and pushed him back in the car. "He's knocked out. I don't think he'll give us any more trouble."

Less than an hour later, Sean and Troy were dropping Norman off at a secure location. Since he executed a jail break from the federal penitentiary, he was now in a tight secure facility. It would take an act of Congress in order for Norman to be transferred. With him being a national security threat, Sean and Troy made the official transfer of their ward.

Sean felt confident that Norman would no longer be a problem. Thanks to the women, the scientist responsible for creating the formula would also be behind bars and away from the general population.

Sean and Troy spent the next few hours debriefing the agents on Norman. They were the same people who had the vials and destroyed them.

One of the agents took them to a room connected to an interrogation room. Through the two-way mirror, they witnessed Braylon being interviewed by another agent.

Braylon wiped the sweat from his brow. "I just did as I was told. I don't know anything about a plan to poison the Dallas water supply."

"He's lying," said the agent in the room with Sean and Troy.

"Regardless, he knew what he was making was deadly. So let him hold on to the lie," Sean said.

The agent opened the door. He was handed a glass of water. The agent took out a vial that looked familiar to Sean and poured the contents of the vial in the water. The agent placed the glass in front of Braylon. "Drink up."

Braylon responded, "I'm not thirsty."

"I said, drink it." The agent picked up the glass and put it up to Braylon's mouth. Braylon switched his head back and forth, keeping his mouth tightlipped.

"Okay. I knew what they planned to do. I needed the money. My mom has cancer and her insurance isn't paying for everything," he blurted.

The agent placed the glass down on the table and listened to Braylon's confession.

"Who ordered this?"

"I spoke to the man himself," Braylon said.

"And who is that?" the agent asked.

"Norman. My father, Norman."

Sean was shocked to learn that Braylon was Norman's son. *No wonder Norman was adamant about us not harming him.*

Sean looked at Troy. "Looks like father and son will have plenty of time to bond."

"Yes, behind bars."

The agent in the room said, "Fellows, we think we got everything we need. There's a phone call for you." The agent hit the speaker button on the phone that was on the edge of the table.

The president's voice coming from the other end of the phone surprised Sean and Troy. "Fellows, thank you both for the outstanding service you've provided not just for the citizens of Dallas, but you went beyond the call of duty and derailed what could have been a national disaster."

Sean stuck his chest out in pride as he listened to the first Black president commend them on a job well done.

~ 37 ~

Montana removed the cucumbers from her eyes. She sat up on the table, making sure the white terry cloth robe was secure. She had just finished getting a full-body massage. She went and sat in the black empty chair in between Savannah and Asia. After the ordeal they had just gone through, the men in their lives surprised them with an all-expenses-paid day at the spa.

Montana released more stress the moment her feet hit the warm, soothing water. Four hours later and stress-free, Montana and her sisters walked out of the spa to the waiting limousine. They each held up wine-filled glasses and cheers.

"To the Blake sisters," they shouted in unison.

Asia leaned back in her seat. "I could live like this every day."

Montana sipped her wine. "I could too. Maybe I need to think about branching out my services so I can make more money."

"Well, I was thinking, maybe we could outsource our services to the government," Savannah said.

Montana and Asia looked in Savannah's direction. Montana said, "I don't know about all of that. I like to keep my life simple. And, ladies, let's face it, this past week has been filled with so much dangerous drama."

"I kind of like it myself. Never boring, that's for sure," Asia said.

"So, what you two saying?" Montana asked.

"I'm going to talk to Troy about using me for more assignments. I don't know how he's going to react since we had a little fallout with this situation, but I kind of like what we do. I feel like we made a difference," Savannah said.

Asia added, "We saved some lives."

"Yes, but still. It was dangerous. If it wasn't for Savannah getting kidnapped and Sean putting himself in danger's way, I can't really say I would have done it."

Asia said, "Come on, Montana. You were enjoying making us up."

"Yes, I did, but that doesn't mean it's something I want to do all of the time. I like my day job."

"Fine," Asia pouted. "Savannah and I will leave you alone about it, if you'll agree to help us out when needed.

"Speak for yourself," Savannah said. "Montana, you can still keep your 'day job' but without you, we wouldn't be able to do this. We need you. Please reconsider."

Montana shrugged. "I'll think about it."

"Great, that's all we ask," Savannah said as she poured herself another glass of wine.

"Hey, driver, you're going in the wrong direction," Asia said when she knocked on the window separating the front from the back.

The driver didn't acknowledge Asia. Savannah picked up the phone. The driver answered. "Didn't you hear my sister? You're going in the wrong direction."

The driver responded, "I have my orders. I will not deviate from them."

Asia said, "What the hell? Stop this thing right now."

The driver pulled off the Monfort exit. Asia tried to open her door but the doors must have had child locks on them because they wouldn't budge. Montana hit the button for the top window but it wouldn't move either.

The limousine pulled into the driveway of what looked like an abandoned building. "Where in the hell are we?" Savannah yelled.

"Nobody's answering their phones," Montana said. She had dialed Sean's, Troy's, and Mike's numbers.

"I didn't even think to bring my weapon," Asia said.

Savannah reached in her purse. She tilted her purse so Asia and Montana could get a good view of her small silver-handle pistol. "I'll never leave home without it again. When the door opens, distract him."

The driver opened up the door and before he could blink, Savannah had the gun pointed at him.

He stuttered, "I don't have any money. Take my ring. Take my watch, but please don't kill me."

Asia said, "What kind of driver are you? Scared of a little gun."

"I didn't sign up for this. I just drive and do my job. Please don't hurt me. I got a wife and kids."

Laughter was heard coming from the sidelines. Montana looked in the direction and saw Sean, Troy, and Mike dressed in slacks and button-down shirts. They walked in their direction.

Troy reached for Savannah's arm. "Put that away." He looked at the driver. "Man, we're sorry. This has been a long week."

Savannah placed the gun to her side.

The driver said, "I understand that, but there's no need to pull out a gun on a brother. I'm trying to help these men surprise y'all. See that's why it doesn't pay to be romantic. Good luck. I got to take off. This was just too much for me. I thought I was going to have a heart attack."

Troy handed him a $200 tip for his trouble. They watched the limousine driver jump in the limousine and speed away. As soon as the tires screeched, they all burst out laughing.

"See y'all wrong. Should at least told one of us something," Montana said.

Sean said, "We were trying to surprise y'all."

"Now you know what happens when you try to surprise us."

"Yes, y'all try to pistol whip a brother," Sean responded, as they all laughed.

~ 38 ~

Sean found himself laughing more and more throughout the night. Things had been so intense and dangerous that it was good to see Montana and her sisters relaxed. He was enjoying everyone's company, but he couldn't wait to get Montana by herself. He loved everything about her: the way she tilted her head when she laughed, the twinkle in her eye when she talked to him. He vowed to do anything he had to do to keep a smile on her beautiful face.

Savannah and Troy were the first to make their excuses to leave. Troy yawned real loud. "I'm so tireddd." He dragged the "d."

Savannah yawned too and added, "Me too."

Sean looked at Montana. "I'm ready if you are."

"Let's go."

Asia looked at Mike. "Don't even think about it. Since my sisters are abandoning me, you can take me home. I don't need you to walk me to my door. Just drop me off."

Mike responded, "I'll drop you off all right. Drop you off right around the corner from your place, that way I won't have to back up."

Asia cut her eyes. Sean laughed. "Come on, baby." Sean held Montana's chair out and extended his hand.

She grabbed it and stood up. "Mike, get my sister home safely."

He responded, "Montana, because I like you and Savannah might shoot me, you can guarantee Asia will get home safely."

Sean and Montana drove home listening to the *The Best of Michael Jackson* CD. They took turns singing lead on the songs that played. Sean felt rejuvenated as they entered Montana's home.

"Thanks for the wonderful day. I've really enjoyed the spa, the limousine ride—well, up until the part I thought he was kidnapping us—and dinner. You guys outdid yourselves."

Sean wrapped his arm around Montana's waist. "I'm glad I contributed to that beautiful smile on your face." Sean planted a kiss on the nape of her neck.

"Mmm. Not so fast. Meet me in my bedroom in about ten minutes." Montana seemed to glide up the stairs.

Sean locked the doors and made sure the house was secure. He wasn't sure if ten minutes had passed and he didn't care. He didn't want to wait a minute more so he made his way up the stairs. He saw the glimmer of the light reflected by the candles that filled the bedroom. Sean smiled.

Montana met him at the door with a sexy black lingerie. She pulled him inside of the room. Instead of waiting for him to respond, she pushed him gently and he fell down on the bed. Montana leaned down and kissed him and that's when Sean took control. He fell back on the bed with her on top of him.

Their lips locked and his manhood was in a tight position. He needed some relief. With his free hand, he unbuckled his pants. Montana saw what he was doing and assisted him. She helped him remove his pants and his shirt. In less than a minute, Sean was naked.

Sean slowly removed the black straps from Montana's shoulders. He planted kisses in each spot. "I've been thinking about this moment all day," he admitted.

"I love you, Sean," Montana said as she stared into his eyes.

Instead of responding with words, Sean wanted to respond with his actions. The lingerie fell to the side of the bed. He kissed Montana from head to toe and then back up again, stopping at the opening of her thighs.

He took her in his mouth and savored her flavor. Montana's thighs gripped him around his neck, but he didn't stop. He wanted to pleasure her until she experienced several orgasms. Satisfied that she had, Sean then devoured her mouth and entered her body with a nice and slow thrust.

Their bodies rocked and were in sync. He tried to control his body but Montana's wetness and moans pushed him over the edge and he came with a force that had him howling like a wolf. He held on to Montana for dear life as they climaxed together.

Sean held Montana in his arms and felt like now was the perfect time to approach her about their future. "Baby, I've been doing a lot of thinking. How do you feel about us?"

Montana responded, "Things have moved fast, but I know what I know and I know that I love you, Sean. And from your performance tonight, I know you love me."

Sean used one of his hands and wiped the hair from in front of her eyes. "Montana, you complete me. I don't want my life to go back to how it was before."

"Sean, I don't plan on going anywhere. I plan on being right by your side."

"So you're my ride-or-die chick?" he teased.

"Well, I guess you can say that," she responded.

"Will you be my wife?" he asked.

"I'll be whatever you want me to be," Montana responded.

"So that's a yes."

"Wait, did you say wife?"

"Montana Elaine Blake, will you marry me?"

"All of this is moving so fast. I can't believe I'm doing this."

Sean had reached over and removed the black velvet box from his pants pocket, but hesitated as he waited for Montana's response.

She continued, "Yes. Sean, I will take a chance and commit to you. But I don't want to rush. There's still things we need to learn about each other."

Sean held the black velvet box in front of her. "Montana, we'll do it your way, baby. Now, if it was up to me, we could go down to the justice of the peace tomorrow."

Montana propped herself up on her elbow. She opened up the box he had been holding. She stared at the princess-cut diamond. "It's absolutely beautiful."

Sean took it out of the box and slipped it on her finger. "Perfect."

"Perfect," Montana repeated what he said. She then kissed him.

They made love throughout the night.

Over breakfast the next morning, Sean said, "I'm serious, Montana. I would marry you today, if you wanted to."

"Let's do it."

Sean wasn't sure he heard her correctly. "Are you sure? I thought all women wanted big, lavish weddings."

"I'm normally not one to do things on the impulse, but in light of everything that's happened, I've learned to stop worrying about what everyone else will think and do things my way. I love you, so why wait? Give me time to find something nice to wear and we can head downtown."

Sean's mouth dropped open when he saw the vision of loveliness staring right back at him. "Montana, you look absolutely beautiful."

"I'm glad you approve," Montana twirled around once showing off the white chiffon ruffled dress that seemed to accent each one of her curves. Her hair was pinned up and the light make-up displayed her natural glow and beauty of her face.

Sean reached his hand out and she grabbed it. "Come. I don't think I can wait a minute longer to make you my wife."

Montana followed Sean out of the house. He called in a few favors as they drove to the courthouse. Sean pulled a few strings and they were able to get their marriage license. While Montana was filling out their forms, Sean had called Mike and Troy.

"Montana, what's going on?" Savannah asked as she and Troy walked in the courtroom, followed by Asia and Mike.

Montana looked at Sean. He said, "Well, this is a special day and I know how much you love your sisters so here they are. Now we can make this thing official."

The bailiff announced the arrival of the judge.

Asia stated, "Oh my goodness. I can't believe these two."

Mike placed his hand over Asia's mouth.

Sean and Montana stood before the judge and exchanged vows.

"By the power of the state of Texas, I now pronounce you husband and wife. You may kiss your bride."

Sean's heart overflowed with love as their lips locked and sealed their union.

Their friends and family congratulated them afterward. Sean heard Savannah tell Montana, "I can't believe you beat me to the altar. If I wasn't so happy for you, I would be jealous."

"I know, right. Sean asked me last night. I just felt it was right."

Since it was all last minute, they all decided to meet up at a local restaurant to celebrate.

Troy stood up and did a toast. Sean refilled both his and Montana's glasses with champagne. He stood up. "This is a new chapter in my life and I'm glad to share it with my brothers." Sean looked at Troy and Mike. "And, my new sisters." He looked at Savannah and Asia. "Montana, I'm proud to have you as my wife and I promise to love and cherish you for the rest of my life."

Montana stood up and they clinked their glasses. Sean took Montana's glass and set it on the table next to his. They tuned out their family and the rest of the restaurant patrons and once again sealed their union with a kiss.

~ 39 ~

The breeze from the ocean swept through the open hotel window, causing a chill to run up and down Montana's spine. The sound of Sean's snoring was like music to her ears. She was enjoying the fifth day of her marriage to a man who swept through her life like a whirlwind. Here they were enjoying their new lives as husband and wife on one of the most beautiful places on the planet, Paradise Island, Bahamas.

She closed her eyes with hopes of drifting off but the chirping of the phone put her thoughts of going to sleep on hold. She reached across Sean. He stirred but didn't wake up. She answered the phone, "Hello." She repeated it several times without a response from the other end.

She placed the phone back on the hook. The phone rang again. Montana answered and still there was no response.

Sean asked, "Who was that?"

"Must have been a wrong number because they didn't say anything."

Sean's eyes shot open. "Put your clothes on," he stated in a firm voice.

Montana didn't move immediately. Sean threw some clothes on the bed. "Come on, Montana, we might not have much time."

"What's going on?" she asked, but while putting her clothes on.

Sean slipped on his jeans and shirt while retrieving a weapon from one of his bags: a gun that Montana had no idea he had with him. He threw some items and her purse that held their important documents in a duffle bag.

Sean grabbed a duffle bag and reached for Montana's hand. "Come on, baby, we need to get out of here."

"Baby, what about our bags?" Montana asked.

"I'll send someone for them later. Now keep it down."

Montana saved her other questions for later. She trusted Sean and slipped out of the patio door of their hotel room at the same time she heard a loud knock at their hotel room door.

Montana held on to Sean's hand as they sprinted to the first available cab driver.

Sean shouted, "Get us to the airport ASAP and I'll give you an extra one hundred American dollars."

The middle-aged cab driver responded, "I got you, mon."

Montana shifted in her seat as the cab driver pulled off as if their life depended on it. And from the look on Sean's face, it just might.

"Do you have a cell phone?" Sean asked the driver.

"For you, mon, yes." The cab driver threw the cell phone to the back while maneuvering the cab around curves.

"This is Sean. There's been a change of plans. We need to get out of here ASAP." Sean paused and then continued, "Thirty minutes? We don't have thirty minutes." Sean went back and forth with the person on the phone.

"We're almost there," the cab driver said, right before his cab got broadsided by a black SUV.

"Hold on," were the last words Montana recalled hearing right before their cab flipped over several times.

"Montana, baby, are you okay?" Sean asked several times.

Montana had blacked out. She slowly came to and blinked her eyes. Her head felt like it was about to fall off. "Where am I?"

"Baby, we need to get out of here before the people in the other vehicle come to. I want you to lean on me."

Montana eased herself up, and felt herself feel faint. Sean caught her. He held the backpack on one shoulder and held her with his other arm.

She gathered up enough strength to stand on her own. "The driver. Is he okay?"

"Baby, he didn't make it."

"Oh, no," Montana moaned.

"Come on. We're not that far from the airport."

They eased into the brush so they wouldn't be able to be seen from the road. All sorts of noises could be heard. If Sean wasn't with her, Montana would be scared out of her mind. She had to trust him so she pushed her fear to the side as they rushed toward the airport.

The approaching headlights of an oncoming vehicle must have spooked Sean. "Get down," he yelled only loud enough for her to hear.

Montana did as instructed. "Baby, my head. It's killing me."

"Hang on in there. We're going to be there any minute. We need to wait for this car to pass us by."

The sound of the car got closer and closer. Montana's heart beat faster and faster. The car eased by them.

"Let's crawl until I'm sure the car is out of sight," Sean instructed.

Montana crawled behind Sean. She didn't want to imagine what her bare hands were touching. Sean stopped and looked behind them. He stood up and helped ease her on her feet.

"Come on, baby, we're almost there."

The sight of the lights of the small airport brought Montana relief.

"Baby, don't look back. I need you to run. Run as if your life depended on it," Sean said as he grabbed her hand and started running toward the waiting small airplane.

Montana made the mistake of looking back and saw the approaching vehicle. Montana ran because her life did depend on it.

Sean stopped and made sure Montana entered the aircraft first. He then entered and with the help of the steward closed the airplane door. Shots were being fired as soon as the plane started rolling down the runway.

Montana squeezed Sean's hand, closed her eyes, and said a silent prayer as the plane ascended in the air.

~ 40 ~

Sean watched Montana drift off to sleep. This was not the way he wanted to start off their marriage. He thought after the situation with Norman he could live a semi-normal life. He should have known not to put his guard down. The steward equipped him with a phone. "Mike, this is Sean. I need you to get someone to sweep my hotel room. Someone tried to kill us."

Sean gave Mike all of the information he would need to get the ball rolling. Sean dialed Troy's number. "Don't want you to alarm Savannah or Asia, but someone tried to kill us. I got Mike working on it now. We're in the air headed to Miami. I need you to get me a car and some equipment ready because it might be a long drive back to Texas. I want to avoid Miami's main airport because whoever is after me will probably look for us there."

Troy responded, "Consider it done. Do you have your cell?"

"Yes. Text all instructions there."

"How's Montana?"

"She's sleeping now but I'm about to wake her up because she has a slight concussion, I think."

"I won't say anything to the girls just yet, but I know I'll need to tell them something."

"I'll let you deal with that. Just get me what I need."

"I'm about to get with Mike so we can find out what's going on."

"In the meantime, you might want to put some protection around the girls too," Sean said.

"I'm already on it, bro. Be safe."

Sean and Troy ended their call. Sean shook Montana gently.

"Baby, we're almost in Miami," Sean informed her.

"Who were those people?" Montana asked.

"I'm trying to find that out now." Sean wished he had more to tell her but he didn't.

"Our life will never be boring I see," Montana jokingly said.

The phone chirped. He saw the caller ID and saw Mike's number displayed. "This is Mike now. Hopefully, he has some news for me," Sean said as he hit the green button.

Sean listened as Mike talked. "All of your stuff is being recovered and will be shipped. We're checking out video now so we can cross-reference and see who these people were."

"I asked Troy to get me a car," Sean said out loud.

"Once you get to Miami, one of our people will be at the small airport. Jack Daniels will be there to escort you back to Dallas," Mike said.

Good ol' Jack. Sean hadn't seen him in a few years but Jack could be ruthless and until he knew who was after him and his wife, he needed someone like Jack to have his back.

Sean responded, "Hit me back when you know something else."

Thirty minutes later, the plane landed. Jack, ten years older than Sean and a few inches taller and wider, was waiting for them at the gate in his black SUV.

"I hear you needed me son," Jack said in his barritone voice.

Sean and Jack gave each other a brotherly hug. "Now more than ever."

Jack looked at Montana. "So this is the woman who got Sean to jump the broom."

Montana extended her hand. Jack shook it and then pulled her into a hug. "Missy. We're family."

"Okay," was all Montana managed to say.

Sean made sure Montana was secure in the black SUV while he sat up front with Jack.

"Man, I heard you had gotten married. She's a beauty, too. Too beautiful for you if you ask me," Jack teased.

"I'm a lucky man. Almost a dead man but lucky."

"Trouble seems to come when we least expect it," Jack said.

"It caught me off guard, but never again," Sean admitted. Sean noticed Montana was unusually quiet. He wondered what was going on in her mind.

Sean's phone chirped, indicating an incoming call.

Mike's voice was on the other end. "Remember Raheem?"

Sean recalled the blast from their past. Raheem was a notorious Texas drug lord. "So Raheem's in the Bahamas?"

"He's not but his brother is. Apparently, he's the one who spotted you and Montana at the airport. They've had you under surveillance ever since you guys showed up there."

Sean cursed out loud before responding to Mike. "Mike, I suggest you heighten up security. I have a feeling that the Bahamas is just a prelude to things to come."

"I knew this day was coming, but I just didn't know when," Mike stated. "Looks like Raheem is coming out of retirement."

"And, Mike, you know he's going to come gunning for you."

"I don't fear death but have a lot to live for," Mike responded.

"Be careful," Sean said, having an uneasy feeling about this new revelation. Sean ended the call and said out loud, "We're safe for now, but something tells me there's a war brewing and we must be ready."

Montana asked, "So you know who tried to kill us?"

"Yes, and he's worse than the devil himself. He makes the devil look like an angel."

"Why do you say that?" Montana asked.

"Mike pulled the trigger that ended the life of Raheem's pregnant wife two years ago. Raheem disappeared off of law enforcement's radar but now it seems he's ready to come out of hiding."

A chill ran down Sean's spine as he read a text from an anonymous number. "A life for a life. Tell Mike."

41

Montana felt a dire need to talk to her sisters after hearing about Raheem. "My phone needs charging. Can I use yours?"

Sean hesitated before responding. "I'm waiting on Troy to call me."

"I know how to click over or hand you the phone," Montana responded.

Sean reluctantly handed her the phone. "Don't tell them where we are."

"That'll be easy because I really don't know where we are."

She dialed Savannah's phone but there was no answer. She clicked the end button and dialed Asia.

"What's up, sis? Surprised to hear from you since you're on your honeymoon," Asia responded.

"For once, can you be quiet and listen?" Montana interrupted.

"Well, excuse me."

"I'm on my way home. Someone shot at us and we had to leave the Bahamas."

Asia shot out question after question.

Montana responded, "That's as much as I can say over the phone. Sis?"

Asia said in a soft voice, "Yes."

"Be careful. You might want to stay clear of Mike until all of this blows over, too."

"What do you mean stay clear of Mike?"

"He's the reason we had to cut our trip short."

Asia asked, "Montana, so exactly what are you saying?"

Sean said, "Montana, don't. Let Mike tell her."

Montana placed her hand over the receiver. "She needs to know." Montana ignored Sean and blurted out, "Mike's life may be in danger. Someone from his past wants revenge and believe me they are no joke."

"No. Please, tell me you're just kidding. Not after Mike and I . . ." Asia's voice trailed off.

"After you and Mike did what?" Montana asked.

"We . . . I can't believe this. I can't do this. I got to go."

Without another word, Asia hung up the phone.

Sean said, "Baby, I wish you would have let Mike tell her."

"But she's my baby sister. I had to say something," Montana responded.

She dialed Savannah's number again and this time Savannah picked up. She repeated to Savannah what she had told Asia. Savannah responded, "I'll check on Asia. Troy's not here. Now I understand why."

"I promise to be in touch. My phone's dead and my charger is in my stuff back in the Bahamas so if you need to reach me, call the number that's showing up on your caller ID," Montana said.

Montana ended the call with Savannah and handed it back to Sean.

She found herself drifting off to sleep. Sean gently shook her and woke her. She wiped her sleeping eyes. It was now nighttime. They were at a gas station that appeared to have a small diner connected to it.

Jack said, "We can gas up, use the restroom, and grab something to eat."

Montana rushed to the restroom at the back of the restaurant. The stares from the patrons didn't intimidate her because her bladder needed relief.

When she exited the restroom, Sean was seated at a booth on his cell phone. She slipped in the seat next to him. He placed his hand on top of hers and squeezed it.

Montana waited patiently for Sean to end his call. She looked out the window and saw Jack putting gas in his SUV.

"Honey, I'm so sorry. Our lives weren't supposed to start off like this," Sean said, now with his arm around Montana's shoulder.

Montana leaned over and kissed him lightly on the lips. "I don't blame you for what's happened in the last twenty-four hours."

Sean sighed. "I thought you regretted your decision."

"Look at me." Sean obeyed her. Montana continued to say, "I married you for better or worse."

Sean added, "Our life will never be boring. That's for sure."

"Exactly. I knew that when I agreed to marry you."

"So no regrets?" Sean asked.

"None, baby. None whatsoever." Montana sealed it with a kiss to reassure him.

Jack walked up to the table and cleared his throat before sitting down. "I almost forgot you were newlyweds."

Montana wiped the lipstick from Sean's lips with her fingers. "I almost forgot myself."

Jack said, "Montana, I promise you, I will not let anyone harm you or this man right here. He's like the son I never had."

Montana smiled. She could tell Sean respected Jack. She had just met him and could tell Jack was a man used to being in control and taking control. Between Sean and Jack, she felt well protected.

She laughed at Jack's jokes about Sean. It was only because of her past experiences did she notice the car slowly pulling up to the gas station and four men who didn't look like your ordinary travelers exit their vehicle.

"Sean, we got company."

Sean didn't hear her at first so she hit his arm. "Ouch," he responded.

"They've found us," Montana said.

Jack yelled, "Let's go."

Jack headed toward the back of the restaurant instead of the front door. She followed him as Sean walked behind them. Murmurs from the restaurant patrons could be heard as Jack led them through the back fire exit door.

"Stay close behind me," Jack said as he held out his black gun.

Montana's heartbeat increased.

Jack held up his hand. Montana stopped in her tracks with Sean on her heels.

Jack whispered, "When I count to three I want you to walk . . . not run to the SUV. Montana, hop in the back and get down."

Jack counted out, "One . . . two . . . three."

Montana increased her pace. It seemed the closer they got the SUV, the farther it got. Montana didn't breathe until she was safely in the back of the car, and the gas station and restaurant was in distant view.

42

Sean kept looking back to make sure Montana was okay. He took his wedding vows seriously. He loved Montana with all of his heart and soul and would give up his life so that she could live if it ever came down to it. It took him a lifetime to find the unconditional love that Montana had freely given him. He would die before allowing anyone to come in between that.

Jack broke Sean's train of thought. "We've lost them, but my instincts tell me that's not the last we will see of them. I think we need to alter our plans. I'll continue driving but I'm going to get you two to an airport. Instead of flying into DFW, I will have you fly into Addison's airport."

Sean agreed. He listened as Jack called and made the arrangements. Three hours later, Sean and Montana were landing at the Addison airport. Addison was in the suburbs of Dallas so Troy was waiting to pick them up.

Before he and Montana could reach Troy's car, Savannah exited the car and ran up to embrace her sister.

"I'm so glad you're okay," Savannah said.

"Ladies, this reunion needs to take place in the car," Sean said, hurrying Montana and Savannah along.

Montana and Savannah sat in the back seat while Troy jumped in the front passenger seat.

"Mike is being stubborn and hard-headed. He's refusing to move to the safe house until we get coordinates on where Raheem is."

"Best believe, he or his people if not already here are on their way to Dallas and they are determined to make not only Mike's life a living hell, but mine too."

"The only reason why they don't know about me is because I was out of the country," Troy said.

"Let's keep it like that."

"I'm sure if they've had Mike under surveillance, I've come up on their radar," Troy said as he drove Sean to Montana's place.

"Asia's not answering her phone," Montana said.

Sean responded, "I'll try Mike."

Savannah added, "I already did. He's not answering his either."

Mike was the one Sean usually called when he wanted to track somebody down. Now, who would track the tracker?

Troy said, "They may be in the safe house. If so, he would have made Asia ditch her phone."

Sean dialed the number to the safe house from Troy's phone. "Where are y'all?" Mike's voice rang from the other end.

Sean sighed. "Man, you had us worried for a minute."

"I had to go swoop up Asia. I'm not sure of how much info they have on me. Asia's the most important thing to me and after fussing and plenty of resistance, I finally convinced her to come with me."

Sean ended the call. "Asia's fine. She's with Mike."

Montana responded, "Being with Mike doesn't make me feel at ease."

Sean didn't know how he was going to break the news to her and Savannah but they would find out soon enough. "It's really not my place to say this but I am. Mike thinks Asia's life could be in danger so he brought her to the safe house with him."

Explicit words flew out of Montana's and Savannah's mouths. Montana said, "I knew it. I knew it from our last conversation."

Savannah asked, "Knew what?"

Montana informed Savannah of what Asia had said. Savannah said, "I don't know if I can keep going through this."

Montana said, "A woman can't help who she falls in love with. Look at us."

Savannah agreed. "But Mike and Asia."

Troy said, "Yeah. I thought they couldn't stand each other."

Sean added, "I saw it coming months ago."

Montana frowned. "And you didn't share this information with me?"

"It's your sister. I thought you knew she had the hots for my boy."

"I'm sure it was the other way around," Savannah responded.

Montana said, "Yes, if anything Mike probably bugged her so much, she felt pity on him."

Sean smiled. "Like you felt pity on me."

"Sean, when I met you, it was lust . . . I mean, love at first sight."

Everyone in the car laughed.

Epilogue

A month later . . .

Montana tried to concentrate on the dinner with her sisters and their men. It had been a month and Raheem and his men hadn't made one move. Although cautious, Mike and Asia went back to a somewhat normal life. Normal as could be under the circumstances.

The dining room was filled with loads of jokes and laughter, but still Montana couldn't keep her mind off of the unknown. Her eyes locked with Sean's. He held a concerned look in his eyes.

Troy said, "Mike, I think you staying at the safe house with Asia for now is a good idea. At least we know getting into it is like Fort Knox."

Mike responded, "I'm really not trying to live my life in fear. If it was just me, I would go confront him head-on." Mike glanced in Asia's direction.

Asia looked up at Mike. "Don't let me be the reason you don't. I'm not living my life in fear."

"Calm down, Asia," Montana said.

"You know your sister. I let her have her say. She'll eventually calm down," Mike said.

"I'm sitting right here," Asia said. "Y'all talking like I'm not in the room."

Mike said, "All I'm saying, Asia, is I want to take precautions until we—meaning Troy, Sean, and I—come up with a plan of action that will put Raheem away for good. He is not the type of person we can just go after. When we do decide to go after him, it will need to be a well-executed plan."

"I understand that, but in the meantime, I'm supposed to put my life on hold? I don't think so." Asia crossed her arms.

"Asia, we would all feel secure if you stayed at the safe house. It's only temporary. The safe house has everything you need. You're here tonight, so it's not like you can't leave and go as you please. You just need to be more aware of your surroundings," Montana said.

"I guess you're right. It's just this situation has me uptight. I like to be carefree. I can't be carefree when I know there's someone out there who wants to kill the man I love," Asia blurted.

"Your man is happy that you're finally admitting that you love him, but baby girl, I'm going to be all right."

Asia calmed down a little. The rest of the dinner went by with idle chitchat, but Montana still couldn't keep her mind off the issue.

Once everyone finished eating, Montana got up to clear the table.

"Need some help, sis?" Asia asked.

"No. I got this. You all sit down," Montana responded as she got up and retrieved the empty plates from the table.

Sean insisted on assisting her with clearing the table. "What's wrong, baby?" Sean asked when they were alone in the kitchen.

"Not knowing when or where this Raheem will decide to strike again has me nervous," Montana admitted.

"Baby, I promise you this, I will give up my life to protect you. I will not let anything happen to you or your sisters."

Montana gently touched Sean on the face. "I know you will. I love you for that. I hope that it never comes to that."

"Let's hope it doesn't. I just want to assure you that I'm going to do my best to keep you safe, so don't worry." Sean squeezed her in his arms.

Montana rested her head on Sean's shoulder, confident that he would protect her by any means necessary.

But her mind drifted to Asia. Would Asia be okay if Raheem came after Mike? What if they tried to get to Asia to get back at Mike? Would Montana be able to deal with that? Those questions and more swam around in her head as she held on to the love of her life as if her life depended on it.

At this very moment it did. Feeling Sean's heart-beat completed Montana's heartbeat as she exhaled.

THE END

Shelia M. Goss is a national bestselling author and a 2012 Emma Award Finalist. She has over fifteen books in print. She writes in multiple genres: Christian fiction, romance, women's fiction, suspense, and young adult. *USA Today* says, "Goss has an easy, flowing style with her prose . . ." Some of her book titles are as follows: *My Invisible Husband* and *Roses are Thorns, Violets are True*, *Paige's Web*, *Double Platinum*, *His Invisible Wife*, *Hollywood Deception*, *Delilah*, *Savannah's Curse*, and *Ruthless*. Her young adult book series The Lip Gloss Chronicles consists of: *The Ultimate Test*, *Splitsville*, *Paper Thin*, and *Secrets Untold*. Besides writing fiction, Shelia is a freelance writer. She's also an *Essence Magazine* bestselling author, the recipient of three Shades of Romance Magazine Readers Choice Multi-Cultural Awards and honored as a Literary Diva: The Top 100 Most Admired African American Women in Literature. To learn more, visit her Web site at www.sheliagoss.com or on Facebook at www.facebook.com/authorsheliagoss.